SUPERVILLAIN!

An Unauthorised and Unofficial Guide to

Dr. Horrible's Sing-A-Long Blog

This edition published in 2018

Text copyright © David Black, David and Sarah Williams

ISBN 978 1 9809 0482 3

This is for Sarah

Contents

INTRODUCTION

During the Writer's Guild Of America strike of 2007 and 2008, Joss Whedon the writer/producer/director/composer/Numfar responsible for creating *Buffy The Vampire Slayer*, *Angel*, *Firefly* and *Serenity* joined forces with his brothers writer Zack Whedon and musician/composer Jed Whedon, as well as his sister-in-law writer/actress Maurissa Tancheroen to create something that would not require industrial action.

It could have been anything.

It wasn't pottery.

It was a superhero internet musical comedy drama called *Dr. Horrible's Sing-A-Long Blog* and more importantly, it was awesome. It was funny, the songs were fantastic and the story had a heart breaking sting in the tail. Or tale, it is a story after all.

This book is not about the making of *Dr. Horrible's Sing-Along Blog* (there is another book that does that much better than I ever could, if you only buy one book about *Dr. Horrible's Sing Along Blog* buy that one), nor is it a continuation of the story (there is yet another book that does that, if you only buy two books about *Dr. Horrible's Sing Along Blog* buy that one as well).

Instead this book is a guide devoted to the fictional world that Dr. Horrible, Penny and Captain Hammer inhabit, sing about, live, die and blog in.

David Black
2018

Dr. Horrible's Sing-Along Blog
Recurring Characters in order of appearance

Dr. Horrible/Billy (Neil Patrick Harris [1-3])
Penny (Felicia Day [1-3])
Moist (Simon Helberg [1-3])
Bad Horse Chorus (Nick Towne, Jed Whedon & Rob Reinis [1-3]/
Jed Whedon, Joss Whedon and Zack Whedon [1[a], 2[a]])
Captain Hammer (Nathan Fillion [1-3]/Joss Whedon [1[b]])
Steve the NBN Newsreader (David Fury [3])
'Kitten' the NBN Newsreader (Marti Noxon [3])
Captain Hammer's groupies (Maurissa Tancharoen, Stacy Shirk &
Steve Berg [3])
Bad Horse (Dobber [3])
Professor Normal (Doug Petrie [3])
Dead Bowie (Jed Whedon [3])
Fury Leika (Liz Vassey [3])
Fake Thomas Jefferson (Drew Goddard [3])
Tie Die (Kate Danson [3])

1) *Dr. Horrible's Sing-Along Blog,* Act I   (July 15, 2008)
2) *Dr. Horrible's Sing-Along Blog,* Act II   (July 17, 2008)
3) *Dr. Horrible's Sing-Along Blog,* Act III   (July 19, 2008)

[a] singing
[b] fisting [c]
[c] It's not as graphic as it sounds, see page 18.

11

NAME
Dr. Horrible's Sing-Along Blog, Act One

FIRST BROADCAST DATE
July 15, 2008, a Tuesday

DURATION
14 Minutes

SYNOPSIS
In order to impress the Evil League of Evil, Dr. Horrible stages a Wonderflonium heist, which turns out to be easier than talking to Penny, the girl of his dreams. In the process, he inadvertently introduces her to his nemesis, Captain Hammer.

FIRSTS & LASTS
First appearance of Dr. Horrible, Penny, Moist, Captain Hammer and the Bad Horse Chorus. First mentions of Bad Horse and the Evil League of Evil.

INFORMATION
The Evil League of Evil is led by Bad Horse. Individuals are entitled to apply to join, but the application process is lengthy. The applications themselves require evaluation, but the actions of applicants are watched and graded by the League. Applicants are required to undertake a heinous crime and a show of force. A murder is considered a plus. Letters of condemnation are considered.

Wonderflonium is a substance that is sensitive to bouncing. It can be used in the construction of a device that freezes time.

The Caring Hands Homeless Shelter is a local homeless shelter. They are looking to expand. There is a petition to use a building that the city is planning to pull down and replace with a parking lot. If the city donated it instead, the shelter would be able to provide 250 new beds, get people off the streets and into job training.

Dooley Park is popular with children. Harris and Frank is a locksmiths in the same neighbourhood as Lalonde Inn.

DR. HORRIBLE

He also goes by the name of Billy. He is an evil scientist and inventor. He blogs a blog, responds to emails submitted by his readers and works with a vocal coach to improve his evil laugh. He has applied to join the Evil League of Evil and this year his application is supported by a letter of condemnation from the Deputy Mayor. He regards Captain Hammer as his nemesis. Johnny Snow recently challenged him to a confrontation at Dooley Park, but Dr. Horrible chose not to attend.

Among his inventions are the Transmatter Ray, the Horrible Van Remote and the forthcoming Freeze Ray. He used the Transmatter Ray to teleport bars of gold from a bank vault, but during the transition the molecules shifted and they came out the other end as a Cumin smelling liquid. The Horrible Van Remote magnetically attaches to a van and allows the user to drive it by remote using a mobile phone-like device. His intention is that the Freeze Ray will be a device that uses Wonderflonium to stop time.

He is in love with Penny, but they haven't really spoken. In place of speech, there was mumbling. He uses the same laundromat as she does and is acutely aware of when she does her laundry.

Dr. Horrible uses the Horrible Van Remote to steals a courier van that is carrying a briefcase of Wonderflonium. He is interrupted by Penny attempting to get signatures for her petition. His heist continues despite the interruption and he signs Penny's petition.

When Captain Hammer arrives and crushes the Horrible Van Remote, Dr. Horrible struggles to regain control of the van in order to stop it running Penny over. Dr. Horrible steals the Wonderflonium from under the nose of a distracted Captain Hammer.

PENNY
She volunteers at The Caring Hands Homeless Shelter and collects signatures for a petition for it.

Penny does her laundry on Wednesdays and Saturdays, occasionally missing Saturdays. Penny frequents the same laundromat as Billy. She is unaware of his feelings for her. She recognises Billy from the laundromat.

Captain Hammer pushes her out of the path of the oncoming van and into a stack of rubbish bags.

CAPTAIN HAMMER
He is Dr. Horrible's nemesis. Captain Hammer crushes the Horrible Van Remote and foils Dr. Horrible's van theft. He pushes Penny out of the path of the oncoming van and into a stack of rubbish bags. Distracted by Penny's gratitude, Captain Hammer is unaware of that Dr. Horrible steals the briefcase of Wonderflonium.

MOIST
He is Dr. Horrible's friend. He moistens things. Moist went on a date with Bait and Switch, he thought he was going end up with Bait, but...

OTHER CHARACTERS
BAD HORSE

He rules the Evil League of Evil with an iron hoof. Bad Horse is also known as the Thoroughbred of Sin. He is known for his terrible death whinny. He communicates via a chorus of three cowboys. Bad Horse seals his mail with a hoofmark and apparently sends it in waterproof envelopes. Bad Horse is evaluating Dr. Horrible's application to join the Evil League of Evil. He recommends a heinous crime, a force of force and a murder to support his application.

2SLY4U

A sarcastic emailer to Dr. Horrible's blog.

JOHNNY SNOW

He is an emailer to Dr. Horrible's blog. Johnny Snow believes himself to be Dr. Horrible's nemesis. He waited at Dooley Park for 45 minutes for a presumably pre-arranged altercation, Dr. Horrible did not arrive. He has ice-based inventions.

DEADNOTSLEEPING

An emailer to Dr. Horrible's blog.

CONFLICT DIAMOND

They told Dr. Horrible about Moist's date with Bait and Switch.

BAIT

Double act with Switch. They went on a date with Switch and Moist. Moist thought he was going to end up with Bait.

SWITCH

Double act with Bait. They went on a date with Bait and Moist. Moist thought he was going to end up with Bait.

SONGS

'Horrible Theme'
Music by Joss Whedon

'My Freeze Ray'
Music and Lyrics by Joss Whedon
Performed by Neil Patrick Harris.

'Bad Horse Chorus'
Music by Jed Whedon and Joss Whedon
Lyrics by Joss Whedon
Performed by Jed Whedon, Joss Whedon and Zack Whedon

'Caring Hands'
Music by Jed Whedon
Lyrics by Maurissa Tancharoen and Jed Whedon
Performed by Felicia Day

'A Man's Gotta Do'
Music and Lyrics by Jed Whedon
Performed by Neil Patrick Harris, Nathan Fillion and Felicia Day

BEST LINES

Dr. Horrible: "Wow, sarcasm. That's original."

Penny: "I was wondering if - if I could just... Hey, I know you."
Dr. Horrible: "Hello. You know me? Cool. I mean - yeah, you do...
Do you?"
Penny: "From the laundromat."
Dr. Horrible: "Wednesdays and Saturdays except twice last
month you skipped the weekend. Or if that was you, could have
been someone else - I mean I've seen you..."

Penny: "I was saying, um, maybe we could get the city to donate
the building to our cause. We would be able to provide 250 new

beds, get people off the streets and into job training so they could... buy rocket packs and go to the moon and become... florists... You're not really interested in the homeless are you?"

Captain Hammer: "It's curtains for you Dr. Horrible. Lacy, gently wafting curtains."

CONTINUITY
None, but then this is Act One.

DEATHS
None.

INFLUENCES & REFERENCES
The title, *Dr. Horrible's Sing-Along Blog*, recalls the 1965 portmanteau horror film *Dr. Terror's House Of Horrors* and the 2001 parody series *Dr. Terrible's House Of Horrible*.

Dr. Horrible's lab is in a real-life home. The house was redesigned to look like a mad scientist's lab in an episode of *Monster House*, a TV series that ran from 2003-2006 and saw people homes renovated along quite stark themes.

During the opening monologue direct to camera, over Dr. Horrible's right shoulder there is an out-of-focus shape that bears quite a resemblance to Serenity, the Firefly class transport vessel from Joss Whedon's earlier work *Firefly* (2002-2003) and *Serenity* (2005). It was later revealed to simply be a line of pots and pans hanging up in the window.

Dr. Horrible's Sing-A-Long Blog does owe a debt to *Firefly*, however in the form of costume and props. Dr. Horrible's lab coat is the same one that Simon Tam uses to disguise himself as an Alliance doctor in the *Firefly* episode, *Ariel*. Neil Patrick Harris

17

reportedly auditioned for the role of Simon Tam, which ultimately went to Sean Maher.

AT&T is the largest telephone provider in the United States.

MISTAKES
When Dr. Horrible first uses the Horrible Van Remote, the time reads 5:00 PM, following his conversation with Penny it states that the time is 4:57 PM.

When Captain Hammer is riding on top of the van and he crouches down a safety wire is visible to the left side of the frame.

NOTES
Joss Whedon would appear to have a minor florist fixation referencing them in both *Buffy the Vampire Slayer*'s *Dopplegangland* and *Angel*'s *Spin The Bottle*, and both times implying that they are crazy.

A fish doesn't rot from the head.

When Captain Hammer jumps onto the hijacked van, he punches and destroys the Horrible Van Remote. The fist doing the punching was not Nathan Fillion's, but Joss Whedon's.

CREDITS
Dr. Horrible..Neil Patrick Harris
Captain Hammer...Nathan Fillion
Penny ....Felicia Day
Moist ....Simon Helberg
Bad Horse Chorus #1 ....Nick Towne
Bad Horse Chorus #2...Jed Whedon
Bad Horse Chorus #3 ....Robert Reinis
Van Driver ....Otto Penzato

Neil Patrick Harris is best known for playing the title role in *Doogie Howser, M.D.* (1989-1993) and later Barney Stinson in *How I Met Your Mother* (2005-2014), as well as a fictionalised version of himself in the *Harold & Kumar* films (2004-2011). He has also appeared in *Blossom* (1991), *Captain Planet And The Planeteers* (1992), *Quantum Leap* (1993), *Murder, She Wrote* (1993), *Capitol Critters* (1992-1995), *The Outer Limits* (1996), *Starship Troopers* (1997), *Homicide: Life On The Street* (1997), *Stark Raving Mad* (1999-2000), *Will & Grace* (2000), Ed (2001), *Spider-Man* (2003), *Law & Order: Criminal Intent* (2004), *Numb3rs* (2005), *Robot Chicken* (2009), *Cloudy With A Chance Of Meatballs* (2009), *Glee* (2010), *Cloudy With A Chance Of Meatballs 2* (2013), *A Million Ways To Die In The West* (2014), *Gone Girl* (2014), *American Horror Story* (2015) and *A Series Of Unfortunate Events* (2017-2019). He hosted The Oscars in 2015 and wrote a *Choose Your Own Autobiography*.

Nathan Fillion found fame as Joey Buchanan in *One Life To Live* (1995-2007), Johnny Donnelly in *Two Guys, A Girl And A Pizza Place* (1998-2001), Captain Mal Reyolds in *Firefly* (2002-2003) and *Serenity* (2005), Caleb in *Buffy The Vampire Slayer* (2003) and Richard Castle in *Castle* (2009-2015). Other appearances include *Blast From The Past* (1999), *The Outer Limits* (1999), *Dracula 2000* (2000), *King Of The Hill* (2001), *Pasadena* (2002), *Miss Match* (2003), *Lost* (2006), *Slither* (2006), *Drive* (2007), *Robot Chicken* (2007-2014), *Desperate Housewives* (2007-2008), *The Venture Bros.* (2010), *Husbands* (2011), *Much Ado About Nothing* (2012), *American Dad!* (2012), *Monsters University* (2013), *Guardians Of The Galaxy* (2014), *Gravity Falls* (2014-2015), *Community* (2014-2015), *Con Man* (2015-2017) and *A Series Of Unfortunate Events* (2018). He played the other Private Ryan in *Saving Private Ryan* (1998).

Felicia Day played Vi in *Buffy The Vampire Slayer* (2003), Codex in *The Guild* (2007-2013), Fairy in *The Legend Of Neil* (2008-2010), Mag in *Dollhouse* (2009-2010), Holly Marten in *A Town Called Eureka* (2011-2012) and Charlie in *Supernatural* (2012-2018) as well as appearing in *Monk* (2005), *House M.D.* (2008), *Roommates* (2009), *Dragon Age: Redemption* (2011), *Husbands* (2012), *The High Fructose Adventures Of Annoying Orange* (2012-2014), *Con Man* (2015-2017) and *Stretch Armstrong & The Flex Fighters* (2017-2018). She launched a YouTube channel called Geek & Sundry, she blogs a blog and vlogs a Flog. Her autobiography is entitled *You're Never Weird On The Internet (Almost)*.

Simon Helberg found fame playing Howard Wolowitz in *The Big Bang Theory* (2007-2018). He was approximately one half of comedy duo, Derek and Simon. He also appeared in *Sabrina, The Teenage Witch* (2002), *Van Wilder: Party Liaison* (2002), *MADtv* (2002-2003), *Arrested Development* (2005), *Good Night, And Good Luck* (2005), *Joey* (2004-2006), *For Your Consideration* (2006), *Evan Almighty* (2007), *Studio 60 On The Sunset Strip* (2006-2007), *A Serious Man* (2009), *The Guild* (2010), *Kung Fu Panda: Legends Of Awesomeness* (2011-2014), *The Tom And Jerry Show* (2014) and *Florence Foster Jenkins* (2016). He wrote, directed and starred in *We'll Never Have Paris* (2014).

Nick Towne followed his role as Bad Horse Chorus #1 with a performance as a Roulette Dealer in *The Invention Of Lying* (2009). He worked as a writers' assistant on second and third seasons of the TV Series *Deadwood* (2005-2006), in addition to co-writing his own episode, *Amateur Night*. He went on to write for *Preacher* (2016).

In addition to portraying Bad Horse Chorus #2, Jed Whedon appeared in an episode of *It's A Living* (1987) and as Man At Table in the *Dollhouse* series finale. He co-wrote *Dr. Horrible's*

Sing-Along Blog and *Commentary! The Musical*. He has also written episodes of *Drop Dead Diva* (2009), *Dollhouse* (2009-2010) and *Spartacus* (2012-2013). He co-created *Marvel's Agents Of S.H.I.E.L.D.* (2013-2015) and has co-written nineteen episodes to date, with an adorable habit of alternating first billing with Maurissa Tancheroen. He wrote and performed music for *Pootie Tang* (2001), *Suspension* (2008) and *Much Ado About Nothing* (2012). He directed *Commentary! The Musical* and *Do You Wanna Date My Avatar?* (2009). In 2010, he released an album entitled *History Of Forgotten Things* as Jed Whedon And The Willing.

The third part of the Bad Horse Chorus triumvirate, Robert Reinis has appeared in *Manhattan, AZ* (2000), *Just Shoot Me!* (2000-2002), *NYPD Blue* (2005), *Over There* (2005), *NCIS* (2006), *MADtv* (2005-2007), *Jericho* (2007), the American version of *The IT Crowd* (2007), *Desperate Housewives* (2012), *New Girl* (2012), *The New Normal* (2012) and *Marvel's Agents Of S.H.I.E.L.D.* (2015). He also wrote and produced a short film called *Robbers* (2008) and a TV movie called *The Winklers* (2014).

Otto Penzato has appeared in *Diamonds In The Rough* (1996), credited as Michael Penzato, *Good Vs Evil* (1999) and had an uncredited, but recurring role in *Desire* (2006). In *Dr. Horrible's Sing-Along Blog*, he both played the van driver and worked as first assistant director. It is in jobs like the latter that he worked on *Human Nature* (2001), *Ghost World* (2001), *Wrong Turn* (2003), *The Plot To Kill Nixon* (2005), *Desire* (2006), *Sordid Lives* (2008), *Supah Ninjas* (2011-2013), *Happyland* (2014) and *Gortimer Gibbon's Life On Normal Street* (2014-2015).

REVIEW

Act One makes an instant impact. The blogging itself is hilarious and it is wonderfully represented as a piece to camera. The songs are magnificent and somehow both complex and catchy.

The cast are wonderful throughout and Neil Patrick Harris holds the whole thing together with a magnificent performance.

In many a musical, the plot takes a back seat to the characters, whereas here the slimness of the plot is acknowledged and becomes an asset in itself. The love triangle is foregrounded and Dr. Horrible's evil scheme is far less important.

The central trio of characters don't simply fly, but they soar. As Act One progresses you feel as though you know Billy, Penny, Captain Hammer and Moist innately.

The world building that's on offer here is incredibly rich. The fantastical is expertly grounded in the ordinary.

In short, Act One leaves you wanting more.

NAME
Dr. Horrible's Sing A Long Blog, Act Two

FIRST BROADCAST DATE
July 17, 2008, a Thursday

DURATION
13 minutes

SYNOPSIS
Billy and Penny are talking now, but Penny and Captain Hammer are dating now. Penny introduces Captain Hammer and Billy, and the captain reveals to Billy that he knows his secret identity.

FIRSTS & LASTS
First actual conversation between Billy and Penny.

INFORMATION
Los Angeles has a Superhero Memorial Bridge.

The mayor signs over a building to the Caring Hands Homeless Shelter to expand their facilities.

There is a Henchman's Union. Applicants require a certain number of evil hours to join.

DR. HORRIBLE
As a result of Penny and Hammer's relationship, he is bereft. He volunteers in disguise at the homeless shelter to keep an eye on Penny and Captain Hammer, and later follows them on dates.

Over the course of a year, Captain Hammer beat up Dr. Horrible in Spring, Summer, Autumn and Winter, specifically at Christmas.

Dr. Horrible attempted to disrupt the dedication of the Superhero Memorial Bridge by the Mayor with his Freeze Ray, but the Los Angeles Police Department and Captain Hammer were ready for him and the latter threw a car at his head, while the device was still warming up. The LAPD and Captain Hammer are among the viewers of Dr. Horrible blog.

In his lair, Dr. Horrible puts Captain Hammer's photograph on his dartboard. Billy bumps into Captain Hammer at the laundromat. The Captain recognises him.

His current catchphrase boasts that he has "a PHd in Horribleness".

PENNY
She has been turned down for several jobs and fired a few times.

Penny begins dating Captain Hammer. They visit the Caring Hands Homeless Shelter and the park together. Penny and Billy have become friends during their visits to the laundromat. She has read The Toy Collector by James Gunn.

CAPTAIN HAMMER
He doesn't go to the gym, because he's naturally strong and fit. At Captain Hammer's disposal are a command center, a Hammer-cycle and a Ham-Jet.

Over the course of a year, he beat up Dr. Horrible in Spring, Summer, Autumn and Winter, specifically at Christmas. Captain Hammer is among Dr. Horrible's blog's viewers.

He and Penny begin to date. They visit the Caring Hands Homeless Shelter and the park, where the Captain attempts to impress her with his prowess on a pedal boat. He convinces the Mayor to sign over the building to the Caring Hands group as a homeless shelter. Captain Hammer bumps into Dr. Horrible whilst visiting Penny at the laundromat and sees through Billy's lack of disguise.

OTHER CHARACTERS
MOIST
He has no expectation of joining the Evil League of Evil.

BAD HORSE
He is also known as the thoroughbred of sin. In light of Dr. Horrible's failed attempt to attack the Superhero Memorial Bridge, Bad Horse insists that he commit a murder to get in to the Evil League of Evil.

HOURGLASS
She can predict the future. Hourglass has seen that a child in Iowa will grow up to become President of the United States of America. She knows Moist.

SONGS
'Horrible Theme'
Music by Joss Whedon

'My Eyes'
Music by Jed Whedon
Lyrics by Maurissa Tancharoen, Jed Whedon and Joss Whedon
Performed by Neil Patrick Harris and Felicia Day
Guitar by Nick Gusikoff

'Bad Horse Chorus (reprise)'
Music by Jed Whedon and Joss Whedon
Lyrics by Joss Whedon
Performed by Jed Whedon, Joss Whedon and Zack Whedon

'Penny's Song'
Music by Jed Whedon
Lyrics by Maurissa Tancharoen and Jed Whedon
Performed by Felicia Day

'Brand New Day'
Music by Jed Whedon and Joss Whedon
Lyrics by Joss Whedon
Performed by Neil Patrick Harris

BEST LINES

Dr. Horrible: "Hey, this is weird. I ordered one frozen yogurt and they gave me two. You don't happen to like frozen yogurt do you?"
Penny: "I love it."
Dr. Horrible: "What a crazy random happenstance."

Penny: "He's a really good looking guy and I thought he was kind of cheesy at first."
Billy (under his breath): "Trust your instincts."
Penny: "But, he turned out to be totally sweet. Sometimes people are layered like that. There's something totally different underneath than what's on the surface."
Billy: "And sometimes there's a third, even deeper level, and that one is the same as the top surface one. Like with pie."

Penny: "It's like Captain Hammer's always saying..."
Billy: "Right. Him. How are things with Cheesy-On-The-Outside?"
Penny: "Good. They're good. He's... nice. I'll be interested to know what you think of him, he said he might stop by."
Billy: "Stop by here?"
Penny: "Yeah."
Billy: "Oh..."
(He checks for a watch that isn't there)
Billy: "Goodness, look at my wrist. I gotta go!"

Captain Hammer: "You've got a little crush, don't you, Doc. Well, that's gonna make this hard to hear. See, later, I'm gonna take little Penny back to my place. Show her the command center, Hammercycle, maybe even the Hamjet. You think she likes me now? I'm gonna give Penny the night of her life, just because you want her. And I get what you want. See, Penny's giving it up, she's giving it up hard. Cause she's with Captain Hammer. And these..."

(Hammer holds up his fists)

Captain Hammer: "...are not the hammer."

(Hammer momentarily walks out of shot, then returns)

Captain Hammer: "The hammer is my penis."

CONTINUITY

Act Two takes place the week after Act One. Presumably the first laundry scene takes place on a Wednesday, because Billy asks after Penny's weekend, and the second laundry scene is Saturday.

DEATHS

None. Although a hundred foot tall Dr. Horrible squashes Captain Hammer in a dream sequence.

INFLUENCES & REFERENCES

Billy's frozen yoghurt of choice came from Berri Good!

The washing machines in the laundromat were made by Dexter. Not a guy called, but a whole company called Dexter.

Spork is a portmanteau word that combines both spoon and fork.

Mahatma Mohandas Gandhi (1869-1948) was the leader of the independence movement in British-ruled India and advocate of nonviolent civil disobedience.

The Toy Collector is a novel published in 2000, written by James Gunn, director of *Slither* (2006), *Super* (2010) and *Guardians Of The Galaxy* (2014).

Billy's bookcase includes Albert L. Lehninger's *Principles Of Biochemistry* (2nd Edition, 1993), *Physics* by James S. Walker (2nd Edition, 2004) and not one but two copies of both *Harry Potter And The Goblet Of Fire* (2000) and *Harry Potter And The Deathly Hallows* (2007) by J.K. Rowling.

The final image of a colossal Godzilla-sized Dr. Horrible destroying buildings evokes memories of a Godzilla-sized *Godzilla* (1954).

MISTAKES
After his beating at the bridge dedication, Dr. Horrible blogs with a bloodied and bruised left eye. When he visits Penny at the laundromat, he has no injuries.

During the song 'Brand New Day' Dr. Horrible rams all of the darts into the centre of the photograph of Captain Hammer's face on the board. As he walks away in the next shot, the darts are all over the board.

NOTES
According to the script, the park that Penny and Hammer visit is MacArthur Park.

CREDITS

Dr. Horrible..Neil Patrick Harris
Captain Hammer...Nathan Fillion
Penny ....Felicia Day

REVIEW

Things take a darker turn as Act Two invites you to side with the villain by making the hero boorish and unbearable. The superheroics (or lack thereof) are largely replaced by a far more schoolyard nerd versus jock narrative.

The songs take a step up in their intricacy, particularly 'My Eyes' and 'Brand New Day', as real life asserts itself and proves to be just as difficult as anything on a super scale.

On the face of it this is Captain Hammer's Act and Nathan Fillion clearly relishes the opportunity to make Captain Hammer the cheesiest superhero that ever walked the Earth and he is hysterically funny doing so. Not to be outdone, Felicia Day embodies Penny with a fragile charm and manages to convey layers of subtext far beyond what the character says and does.

NAME
Dr. Horrible's Sing-A-Long Blog, Act Three

FIRST BROADCAST DATE
July 19, 2008, Saturday

DURATION
16 minutes

SYNOPSIS
The dedication ceremony for the homeless shelter becomes a Captain Hammer ego-fest until Dr. Horrible turns up and graves the day. Penny pays the price, but Billy discovers the cost of getting what you want.

FIRSTS & LASTS
First appearance of the NBN Newsreaders, the groupies, Bad Horse, Professor Normal, Dead Bowie, Fury Leika, Fake Thomas Jefferson and Tie Die.

INFORMATION
NBN News on television, and both The Midtown Metro-Journal and The Informer in print, readily report on the exploits of Captain Hammer.

DR. HORRIBLE
He has converted his Stun Ray into a Death Ray. Dr. Horrible attacks the opening of the new homeless shelter and shoots Captain Hammer with his Freeze Ray. He freezes the Captain, but fails to kill him before the charge runs out and the Captain in unfrozen. Hammer punches him across the room and picks up his Death Ray. Horrible sees that it is damaged and tries to warn Hammer not to use it. He doesn't listen and the Death Ray explodes, causing Hammer pain and fear from the public which Dr. Horrible enjoys, and Penny's death, which he doesn't.

After the attack on the dedication of the homeless shelter, a newspaper dubs him the 'Worst Villain Ever'. Dr. Horrible develops and wears a new arm mounted cannon. He and Moist rob a bank.

Dr. Horrible throws a party, inviting Moist, Pink Pummeler, Purple Pimp and the Bad Horse Chorus among others. Captain Hammer's fan trio defect and become Dr. Horrible fans. He joins the Evil League of Evil and begins wearing a red version of his usual outfit.

PENNY
Penny doesn't eat meat. She and Captain Hammer had sex. Penny is not popular with Captain Hammer's fans.

She attends the opening of the homeless shelter. During Captain Hammer's address to the public, she leaves the stage in embarrassment.

Penny is killed by shrapnel from the Death Ray explosion. Her death is reported in The Mid-Town Metro-Journal.

CAPTAIN HAMMER
Captain Hammer has a trio of superfans. One of whom has a signed photo of him, a lock of his hair and his dry cleaning bill. He owns at least four sweater vests and has them dry cleaned. Captain Hammer and Penny had sex. He has never had sex with the same girl twice.

Regarding the donation of a building by the city to the Caring Hands group, Captain Hammer tells the press he hopes to set an example for children. There will be a statue of him at the new homeless shelter.

At the dedication ceremony, Dr. Horrible shoots Captain Hammer with his Freeze Ray, freezing him in time. The effects wear off just in time for the Captain to punch Dr. Horrible clear across the room and take his death ray from him. He attempts to shoot Horrible with the malfunctioning Death Ray. The Death Ray explodes and Captain Hammer feels pain for the first time. He flees from the scene.

After the incident at the Homeless Shelter, he is "unavailable for comment" to the media for the first time ever and goes into therapy. Captain Hammer's fans shift their allegiance and become Dr. Horrible fans.

OTHER CHARACTERS
MOIST
He is friends with the Pink Pummler. Moist and Dr. Horrible rob a bank. He attends the party at Dr. Horrible's lab.

CAPTAIN HAMMER'S GROUPIES
They are a trio of Captain Hammer fans. Two are female, while the third is male. They wear T-shirts with Captain Hammer's face on. One of them has a signed photograph of Captain Hammer, a lock of his hair and his dry cleaning bill. They are not keen on Penny.

Following Dr. Horrible's attack on Captain Hammer at the homeless shelter, they change their allegiance and become Dr. Horrible fans. They begin wearing T-shirts with Horrible's face on.

THE MAYOR OF LOS ANGELES
The Mayor of Los Angeles dedicates the new building for use as homeless shelter. He was also due to unveil a statue of Captain Hammer, but an attack by a supervillain prevented it.

PINK PUMMELER
He is friends with Moist. Pink Pummeler has a large collection of stuffed toys. He attends the party at Dr. Horrible's lab.

PURPLE PIMP
He is a villain. Purple Pimp attends the party at Dr. Horrible's lab.

BAD HORSE
His chorus attend the party at Dr. Horrible's lab. Bad Horse permits Dr. Horrible to join the Evil League of Evil.

PROFESSOR NORMAL
He is a member of the Evil League of Evil.

FAKE THOMAS JEFFERSON
He is a member of the Evil League of Evil. Not to be confused with the real Thomas Jefferson.

TIE-DIE
She is a member of the Evil League of Evil.

DEAD BOWIE
He is a member of the Evil League of Evil.

FURY LEIKA
She is a member of the Evil League of Evil.

SNAKE BITE
She is a member of the Evil League of Evil.

SONGS
'Horrible Theme'
Music by Joss Whedon

'So They Say'
Music by Jed Whedon and Joss Whedon
Lyrics by Joss Whedon
Performed by Robert Reinis, Zack Whedon, Maurissa
Tancharoen, Stacy Shirk, Steve Berg, Felicia Day, Nathan Fillion,
David Fury, Marti Noxon and Neil Patrick Harris

'Everyone's A Hero'
Music and Lyrics by Joss Whedon
Performed by Nathan Fillion
Backing Vocals by Stacy Shirk and Maurissa Tancharoen
Piano by Danny Chaimson

'Slipping'
Music and Lyrics by Joss Whedon
Performed by Neil Patrick Harris

'Everything You Ever'
Music and Lyrics by Joss Whedon
Performed by Neil Patrick Harris
Bridge by Jed Whedon
Backing Vocals by Maurissa Tancharoen

'Horrible Credits'
Music by Jed Whedon
Violin by Amir Yaghmai

BEST LINES
Female News Anchor: "It's a good day to be homeless."

Male News Anchor: "Next up, who's gay?"

Captain Hammer (reading from a set of tiny cue cards): "I hate
the homeless..."
(next cue card)

Captain Hammer: "...ness problem that plagues our city."

Captain Hammer: "Give my regards to St Peter...or whoever does his job...but in hell."

Mayor Hankins: "Justice has a name! And the name it has...besides 'Justice'...is Captain Hammer!"

Captain Hammer (singing 'Everyone's A Hero'): So I thank my girlfriend Penny. Yeah, we totally had sex. She showed me there's so many different muscles I can flex. There's the deltoids of compassion, there's the abs of being kind. It's not enough to bash in heads, you've got to bash in minds.

Captain Hammer (after the Death Ray explosion) "Oh, I'm in pain. I think this is what pain feels like."

CONTINUITY
The Mayor's dedication ceremony mentioned in Act Two takes place here.

DEATHS
One. Penny is killed by shrapnel from the explosion of the Death Ray.

INFLUENCES & REFERENCES
Captain Hammer mentions Lassie, the canine lead character of film, radio and television in the lyrics of 'Everyone's A Hero.'

The sound effect that indicates when the freeze ray dies is the same as the engine of the Millennium Falcon in *Star Wars: Episode V - The Empire Strikes Back* (1980).

Dr. Horrible's Stun Ray, which he later turns into a Death Ray, is the sonic rifle gun carried by Alliance troopers in the *Firefly* episode, *Ariel* (2002), but held upside-down.

MISTAKES

Dr. Horrible plants the darts in the middle of the dartboard (and the middle of Captain Hammer's photo), he moves to his chair and the darts are once more scattered on the board.

The Mid-Town Metro Journal headline announcing Penny's death is grammatically incorrect: "Heroes Girlfriend Murdered" should read "Hero's Girlfriend Murdered". Presumably the error can be attributed to grief.

Dave Smart, the Bestboy Grip is listed in the credits as "Bestbot Grip".

NOTES

According to the script, the mayor's name is Hankins. There really is a Mayor of Los Angeles and in 2008 the encumbent was James K. Hahn.

CREDITS

Dr. Horrible	Neil Patrick Harris
Captain Hammer	Nathan Fillion
Penny	Felicia Day
Moist	Simon Helberg
Bad Horse Chorus #1	Nick Towne
Bad Horse Chorus #2/Dead Bowie	Jed Whedon
Bad Horse Chorus #3/Moving Guy	Robert Reinis
Mayor	Richard Partlow
Groupie #1	Maurissa Tancharoen
Groupie #2	Stacy Shirk
Groupie #3	Steve Berg
Newsman	David Fury

```
Newswoman .................................................................Marti Noxon
Other Moving Guy ................................................. Michael Boretz
Hawaiian Shirt Guy ........................................... Lance W. Lanfear
Pink Pummeler ....................................................Michael Canaan
Purple Pimp ...........................................................Jonathan Reilly
```

And Introducing the Evil League of Evil:

```
Professor Normal ........................................................Doug Petrie
Fake Thomas Jefferson............................................Drew Goddard
Tie-Die........................................................................Kate Danson
Fury Leika .....................................................................Liz Vassey
Snake Bite..............................................................Athena Demos
Bad Horse.........................................................................Dobber
```

As an actor, Richard Partlow appeared in *Knight Rider* (1986), *The Twilight Zone* (1986) and *Diagnosis Murder* (1994), but he has also made a career as a foley artist on the like of *Bakersfield P.D.* (1993-1994), *The Secret World Of Alex Mack* (1994-1998), *The World Is Not Enough* (1999), *Malcolm In The Middle* (2000-2003), *Battlestar Galactica* (2003-2007), *That 70's Show* (2002-2006), *Scrubs* (2006-2007), *Smallville* (2001-2010), *Marvel's Agents Of S.H.I.E.L.D.* (2013-2016) and uncredited on *Buffy the Vampire Slayer* (1997).

Maurissa Tancharoen played Kilo in *Dollhouse* (2009-2010), Alina in *The Guild* (2011) and Kana in *Mortal Kombat: Legacy* (2011-2013). She has also appeared in *Moonwalker* (1988), *King Of The Hill* (2005), *Much Ado About Nothing* (2012). She wrote six episodes of *Dollhouse* (2009-2010), and fifteen of *Marvel's Agents Of S.H.I.E.L.D.* (2013-2017) to date. She also served as story editor on *Drop Dead Diva* (2009), co-producer on *Spartacus: Gods Of The Arena* (2011) and *Spartacus* (2012), and as Executive Producer on *Marvel's Agents Of S.H.I.E.L.D.* (2013-2017).

Stacy Shirk was cast as Groupie #2 when Joss Whedon saw her performance on stage as Eponine in *Les Miserables*. She went on to appear Whedon's *Much Ado About Nothing* (2012) and *One Day: A Musical* (2014).

Prior to his appearance as Groupie #3, Steve Berg featured in *Free Ride* (2006), *Girlfriends* (2006) and *The Game* (2007). Post-Groupie work includes *Rizzoli & Isles* (2010), *Coogan Auto* (2013), *Drunk History* (2013), *The Goldbergs* (2016-2018), *Idiotsitter* (2016) and *New Girl* (2016). As a writer, he was written *Robbers* (2008), *Skinwalker Ranch* (2013) and *Friends Without Benefits* (2014).

David Fury made a pair of very memorable appearances in *Buffy The Vampire Slayer* (2001-2002) as a man eager to express his amazement at the quality of Sunnydale's dry cleaning, alongside this he also wrote seventeen episodes, performed in a trio of *Angel* episodes (2001-2004) and wrote eleven. He has written instalments of *Lost* (2004-2005), *24* (2006-2010, 2014), *Terra Nova* (2011), *Fringe* (2011-2012), *Homeland* (2015), *24: Legacy* (2017), *The Tick* (2017) and *Lethal Weapon* (2018).

Marti Noxon wrote twenty-four episodes of *Buffy The Vampire Slayer* (1998-2003) and sang in two of them. She also wrote episodes of *Angel* (1999), *Mad Men* (2008-2009), *Private Practice* (2007-2008), *Grey's Anatomy* (2007) and *Glee* (2011-2012). She created and wrote for *Point Pleasant* (2005-2006), *Girlfriend's Guide To Divorce* (2014-2016), *UnReal* (2015-2016) and *Dietland* (2018). At the time of publication, her twitter bio reads "I ruined Buffy and I will RUIN YOU TOO". She is wrong about the former, but only time will tell about the latter.

Michael Boretz served as Joss Whedon's assistant from 2002 to 2003 across *Buffy The Vampire Slayer*, *Angel* and *Firefly*, and then again for *Serenity* (2005). He also worked on *Rollerball* (2002), *Sex And The City* (2002), *Stuart Little 2* (2002) and *Project Runway* (2008).

Lance W. Lanfear worked on most of the *Mystery Woman* TV movies between 2003 and 2006, *Supah Ninjas* (2011-2013) and *Fred* (2012) of which he also directed three episodes.

Michael Canaan appeared in *24* (2003), *Monk* (2004), *Veronica Mars* (2005), *The Bold And The Beautiful* (2008) and *Friends With Benefits* (2011).

Jonathan Reilly owned the house in which the scenes set in Dr. Horrible's lab were shot. In addition to playing Purple Pimp, he also appeared in *I Wanna Be Doctor Who-d* (2011).

Doug Petrie wrote two episodes of *Angel* (1999-2000) and seventeen of *Buffy the Vampire Slayer* (1998-2003). He also wrote for *Tru Calling* (2003-2004), *The 4400* (2005), *American Horror Story* (2013-2014), *Marvel's Daredevil* (2015-2016) and *Marvel's The Defenders* (2017).

Drew Goddard wrote five episodes each of *Buffy the Vampire Slayer* (2002-2003) and *Angel* (2003-2004) as well as writing for *Lost* (2005-2008), *Cloverfield* (2008), *The Martian* (2015), *Marvel's Daredevil* (2015-2016) and *Marvel's The Defenders* (2017). He also wrote and directed *The Cabin In The Woods* (2012). He also appeared in *Much Ado About Nothing* (2012).

Kate Danson has appeared in *Raising The Bar* (2008-2009), *The Protector* (2011) and *CSI: Crime Scene Investigation* (2013-2014).

Liz Vassey has appeared in the likes of *Star Trek: The Next Generation* (1992), *All My Children* (1990-1992), *Quantum Leap* (1991-1993), *ER* (1994), *Pig Sty* (1995), *Maximum Bob* (1998),

The Tick (2001-2002), *Tru Calling* (2005), *CSI: Crime Scene Investigation* (2005-2010), *Castle* (2011) and *9ine* (2011).

Athena Demos also appeared in *Battlestar Galactica: The Second Coming* (1999), *The Practice* (2003), *Sugar Boxx* (2009) and *Tales Of Morrissa* (2017).

Zack Whedon has a cameo as a paramedic taking dead Penny away. He worked on *Angel* (1999), *Deadwood* (2004-2006), wrote for *Fringe* (2008-2009), appeared in *Much Ado About Nothing* (2012) and both wrote and directed *Come And Find Me* (2016).

After a memorable performance as Bad Horse, Joss Whedon was sure to want to work with Dobber again and sure enough when *Dollhouse* needed an equine superstar it was to Dobber they turned.

REVIEW

Act Three ups the ante considerably. Gone are the beautifully constructed references to an outside world and in their place is an outside world that feels perfect. New characters broaden out the scope of the story considerably and the actors all do a fantastic job. Richard Partlow as the Mayor, Maurissa Tancharoen, Stacy Shirk and Steve Berg as the Groupies and David Fury and Marti Noxon as the News Anchors are all incredibly funny and achieve a huge amount with relatively little screen time.

Acts One and Two have made us love the villain and love to hate the hero, Act Three sees the bad guy beat the good guy and we're OK with that, but it all comes at a cost: Penny's death is astounding and tragic.

'So They Say' is a wonderful and sophisticated song, 'Everyone's A Hero' is a great vehicle for Nathan Fillion and ending on 'Everything You Ever' leaves the audience as hollow and numb as Dr. Horrible.

So Dr. Horrible wins the day and gets everything he thinks he wants at the expense of what he actually wants. It shouldn't be this satisfying a viewing experience. How can something leave its audience equally satisfied and bereft? Can you be satisfyingly bereft? Or bereftingly satisfied?

Clearly, yes you can.

FULL CREW LISTING FOR ALL THREE ACTS

Directed by..Joss Whedon
Written by...Joss Whedon
....Zack Whedon
....Maurissa Tancharoen
....Jed Whedon
Produced by..David M. Burns
....Michael Boretz
....Joss Whedon
Director of Photography .... Ryan Green
Editor ....Lisa Lassek
Music by...Joss Whedon
....Jed Whedon
Lyrics by ....Joss Whedon
....Jed Whedon
....Maurissa Tancharoen
Score and Orchestration by ....Jed Whedon

Stunt Coordinator ....Mike Massa
Additional Stunt Coordinator ....Todd Warren
Dr. Horrible Stunt Doubles...Hank Amos
....Justin Woods
Penny Stunt Double ....Stacey Carino
Captain Hammer Stunt Double...................................Mike Massa
....Bill Leaman
Utility Stunts..James M. Churchman
....Paul Leonard
....Kevin Foster

Crew
Unit Production Manager.......................................David M. Burns
1st Assistant Director..Otto Penzato
2nd Assistant Director..Lance W. Lanfear
Camera Operators...Matt Egan
....Ari Gertler

44

Steadicam Operator/Dit...Jeffrey Clark
Steadicam Operator ....Dan Copland
1st Assistant Cameras ....Michael Skor
....Michelle Mann
2nd Assistant Cameras ....Mark Bain
....Shaun Mayor
Dit Technician..Brandon Clark
Gaffer ....Matt Gulley
Bestboy Electrician .... Chuck DeRosa
Key Grip ....Robert McFall
Bestbot Grip ....Dave Smart
Griptricians... Adam Sheedy
....Dave Starks
Production Mixer... Dick Hansen
Boom Man...Michael Kaleta
Set Decorator ....Sandy Struth
Assistant Set Decorator...Ethan Goodwin
Art Director ....Alethea Root
Property Master ....Laura Barker
Property Assistant...Lean Mann
Illustrator..Phillip Boutte
Costume Designer ....Shauna Trpcic
Assistant Costume Designer ....Cleo Mannell

Makeup/Hair Supervisor ....Vickie Mynes
Makeup/Hair ....Keston Ridley
Makeup/Hair Assistants...................................Elizabeth Villamarin
....Nicole True Armstrong

Location Manager..Gabriel Ynda
Script Supervisor..Nirvana Adams
Still Photographer..Amy Opoka
Key Production Assistant.....................................Harry Fitzpatrick
Production Assistants ....Laura Kasek
....Katherine Darrah

.... Dave Trachtenberg
.... T.J. Rotell
.... Benjamin Smith
.... Amy Smith
.... Kira Schlitt
Assistant To Joss Whedon .... Natalie Farrell
Extras Casting by .... Sande Alessi Casting
.... Kristan Berona
.... Robbyn Kraft
Bad Horse Provided by .... Phil's Animal Rentals
.... Phil Smith
.... Marnie Hoffman

Catering by .... Bruce's Gourmet Catering
.... Kristin Nelson
.... Cesar Aliste
.... Coreyce Long
.... Amelia Syhapanha
Craft Service.. Megan Bassin
Fire Safety Officer .... John Sopko
Set Medic.. Yvette Gurrola

Honeywagon Driver.. Rubin Salazar
Generator Driver .... Jeremy McClain
Art Truck Driver .... Fred Sanchez
Assistant Editor .... Carmelo Casalenuovo
Post-Production Consultant.. Aaron Miller
Sound Supervisor and Re-Recording ...... Geoffrey G. Rubay, MPSE
Assistant Sound Editor .... John Cannon
Dialog Editor .... Jason George
Foley Editor... Josh McHugh
Foley Mixer.. Brett Voss
Foley Artist .... Diane Marshall

Additional Musicians.. Danny Chaimson
....Nick Gusikoff
....Amir Yaghmai
Visual Effects by..Zoic Studios
Visual Effects Supervisor ....Michael D. Leone
Visual Effects Producer.......................................Barbara Genicoff
Visual Effects Coordinator ....Sean Tompkins
Online and Color Correction by ....Level 3 Post
End Credits by...Framework Studio

With A Very Special Thanks To.......................................Ben Edlund
....Andrew Fenaday
....Joel Landson
....Loni Peristere
....Tommy Tancharoen
....Robert Glass
....Adam Hauck
....Bill Augustine
....Benji Samit
....Kevin Tancharoen

Dr. Horrible Interrupts The Emmys
Recurring Characters in order of appearance

Dr. Horrible/Billy (Neil Patrick Harris [4])
Captain Hammer (Nathan Fillion [4])
Penny (Felicia Day [4])
Moist (Simon Helberg [4])

4) The 61st Emmy Awards (September 20, 2009)

NAME

None, but *Dr. Horrible Interrupts The Emmys* pretty much covers it.

FIRST BROADCAST DATE

September 20, 2009, a Sunday

DURATION

3 Minutes

SYNOPSIS

Dr. Horrible interrupts the television broadcast of the 61st Primetime Emmy Awards ceremony to demonstrate the superiority of the internet, but Captain Hammer and poor connectivity defeat him.

FIRSTS & LASTS

Last appearances, to date, of Neil Patrick Harris as Dr. Horrible, Nathan Fillion as Captain Hammer, Felicia Day as Penny and Simon Helberg as Moist. This is the last time that Neil Patrick Harris plays himself in a work associated with *Dr. Horrible's Sing-Along Blog*.

INFORMATION

Dr. Horrible's Sing-Along Blog has been nominated for a Primetime Emmy Award.

DR. HORRIBLE

He hijacks the broadcast of the Primetime Emmy Awards. He regards Neil Patrick Harris as an athletic yet luminous host. His Blog has been nominated for an Emmy and he is confident of winning. Captain Hammer intervenes and hits him. The method of his signal intrusion comes unplugged and the battery runs out, allowing the intended broadcast to continue as planned.

PENNY

She is honoured to be nominated for an Emmy.

CAPTAIN HAMMER

He interrupts Dr. Horrible's interruption of the Emmys. He also interrupts Dr. Horrible's face with his fist and elbow. Hammer claims to have mastered the internet. He likes television and is assured that it will be around forever. Hammer prefers CSI: Miami, to the other two. He is honoured to be nominated for an Emmy.

MOIST

He is honoured to be nominated for an Emmy.

OTHER CHARACTERS
NEIL PATRICK HARRIS

He is the presenter of the 61st Primetime Emmys. Harris claims to be excited by the process of tabulating Emmy votes.

ANDY SALE, MIKA VELGA AND JOHN NEMDIC

They are accountants from Ernst & Young. They are often asked to explain the process of tabulating Emmy votes. Neil Patrick Harris invites them onstage to explain for the benefit of the audience, but Dr. Horrible interrupts the broadcast.

SONGS

'The Internet Is...'
Music and Lyrics by unknown
Performed by Neil Patrick Harris.

'It's An Honour To Be Nominated...'
Music and Lyrics by unknown
Performed by Neil Patrick Harris, Nathan Fillion, Felicia Day and Simon Helberg.

BEST LINES
Captain Hammer (facing just off camera): "Don't worry America, I've mastered this internet and I tell you-"
Dr. Horrible: "You have to look into-"
Captain Hammer (correcting his eyeline): "...it's nothing but a fad. TV is here to stay."

Captain Hammer: "People will always need big, glossy, shiny, gloss-covered entertainment "
Dr. Horrible: "But the most important-"
Captain Hammer: "...and Hollywood will be there to provide it. Like the Ottoman Empire, the music industry and Zima we're here to stay."

CONTINUITY
None.

DEATHS
None.

INFLUENCES & REFERENCES
The Emmy Awards are presented by the Academy of Television Arts & Sciences (ATAS) since 1949. In 1974 they were separated out into Primetime and Daytime categories.

Ernst & Young was one of the 'Big Four' accounting firms, founded in 1989 after a merger of Ernst & Whinney and Arthur Young & Co. In 2013 it branded itself as EY.

Probably the most famous example of broadcast signal intrusion took place in 1987, when a scheduled broadcast in Chicago of a *Doctor Who* story called *Horror Of Fang Rock* was interrupted by a transmission of a man in a *Max Headroom* mask. The individuals responsible were never identified.

The Tonys is a nickname for the Antoinette Perry Awards for Excellence in Broadway Theatre. Neil Patrick Harris went on to win one in 2014 for his performance in *Hedwig And the Angry Inch*.

CSI: Miami is a police procedural TV show that ran from 2002 to 2012. It was broadcast opposite *Castle* featuring Nathan Fillion. "The other two" refers to the original *CSI: Crime Scene Investigation* (2000-2015) and spinoff series, *CSI: NY* (2004-2013).

The Ottoman Empire was founded at some point in the thirteenth century AD and finally fell apart in 1922.

The music industry has struggled to move with the times and changes in technology. Illegal downloads have shaken the foundations of the business model of record companies.

Zima is an alcoholic beverage first brought to the marketplace in 1993 and due to poor sales its production in the USA came to an end in 2008. It is still available in Japan.

MISTAKES
Wait, I thought Penny was dead...?

NOTES
Dr. Horrible's Sing-Along Blog did indeed win the Emmy for outstanding special class short format live action entertainment program and Joss Whedon's acceptance speech was gloriously thus: "Thank you, we are honoured to accept the award for most incomprehensible category. This is our small proof, not only that things can be done differently in this business, but that the greatest expression of rebellion is joy. Thank you."

Since the broadcast of this award ceremony sketch, television has been increasingly threatened by internet services like Netflix, Hulu, Amazon Prime etc.

CREDITS

Dr. Horrible..Neil Patrick Harris
Captain Hammer...Nathan Fillion
Penny ....Felicia Day
Moist ....Simon Helberg

REVIEW

This is not the sequel we were hoping for, but there are some positives on offer here. It's great to see our four main characters back and two of them effortlessly back in character as well.

Neither of the songs make it past a single line, so it's difficult to comment on their quality. The jokes are not up to the standard of the Acts One, Two or Three, but it is still a nice tip of the hat to the Sing-Along Blog.

FROM BAD HORSE TO DARK HORSE...AND BACK AGAIN

Dr. Horrible Comics
Recurring Characters in order of appearance

Captain Hammer [1-5]
Captain Hammer's groupies [1, 4]
Steve, the NBN Newsreader [1, 5]
Kitten, the NBN Newsreader [1, 5]
Dr. Horrible [1-4]
Moist [2, 4]
Wingspan [3, 5]
Penny [3, 4]
Professor Normal [5]
Tie Die [5]
Bad Horse [4, 5]
Fury Leika [5]
Fake Thomas Jefferson [5]
Dead Bowie [5]
Bad Horse Chorus [5]

1) *Captain Hammer (Nemesis Of Dr. Horrible): Be Like Me!*
   (July 1, 2008)
2) *Moist: Humidity Rising*   (December 3, 2008)
3) *Penny: Keep Your Head Up*   (June 4, 2009)
4) *Dr. Horrible* One-Shot   (November 18, 2009)
5) *The Evil League Of Evil*   (September 21, 2010)

NAME
Captain Hammer (Nemesis Of Dr. Horrible!): Be Like Me!

FIRST RELEASE DATE
July 1, 2008
Released online in *Myspace Dark Horse Presents* Issue #12.

DURATION
8 pages

SYNOPSIS
Captain Hammer waxes lyrical about heroism, evil and vigilance.

FIRSTS & LASTS
The first comic based on *Dr. Horrible's Sing-A-Long Blog* features the first appearances in comics of both Captain Hammer and Dr. Horrible.

INFORMATION
A park in Los Angeles holds open air signings.

CAPTAIN HAMMER
He was born with a full head of hair and the ability to bench press five hundred pounds. Captain Hammer thwarts robberies, attends movie premieres, visits schools, wins bar fights and is interviewed on television. He advocates controlled fires for children and signs autographs at events. At one such organised signing, he spots Dr. Horrible in the queue and foils his attempt to neutralize the Captain's muscle. He destroys the Doctor's gun.

Captain Hammer regards being able to see trouble before it starts as one of the most important aspects of heroism. He suspects teenage goths and those that excel in science and math of becoming future super villains. He encourages members of the public to report individuals with these attributes to the authorities or risk imprisonment themselves.

OTHER CHARACTERS
DR. HORRIBLE
He creates a gun that is designed to neutralize muscle and intends to use it to weaken Captain Hammer. Dr. Horrible queues up to get Captain Hammer's autograph and/or kill him. He is foiled by the captain and punched high into the air.

BEST LINES
Hammer: "You have to have eyes like a hawk and a mind like a cardiologist to process what your hawk-eyes see...evil lurks everywhere...often in plain sight...Can you lurk in plain sight? Or is that just walking? Oh well, leave it to the cardiologists to puzzle that one out."

CONTINUITY
This comic strip is set before the events of *Dr. Horrible's Sing-A-Long Blog*. Other than Captain Hammer and Dr. Horrible, the other characters from the Blog that also appear here are Captain Hammer's groupies and the NBN Newsreaders from Act Three.

DEATHS
None, probably. Assuming that the trio of thugs Hammer beats up in the opening montage, don't perish.

INFLUENCES & REFERENCES
When Captain Hammer attends the film premiere; he does so in a white tuxedo akin to Sean Connery's James Bond in *Goldfinger*, although without the red carnation. The panel that sees Hammer stood atop a building looking out over the city is an oft-repeated image of heroism whether it is the eponymous hero of *Batman* in Gotham or Captain Jack Harkness from *Torchwood* in Cardiff.

MISTAKES

The comic strip was initially uploaded to *Myspace Dark Horse Presents* Issue #12 a day early and hastily removed.

The later reprint omits the excellent bracketed subtitle: *(Nemesis Of Dr. Horrible!)* and are all the poorer for it.

NOTES

Later printed in *Myspace Dark Horse Presents* Volume 2 and *Dr. Horrible And Other Horrible Stories*.

CREDITS

Written by ....Zack Whedon
Drawn by..Eric Canete
Colored by ....Dave Stewart
Lettered by ....Blambot's Nate Piekos
Created by ....Joss Whedon

Eric Canete is an artist who has worked in comics on *The New Avengers*, *Fear Itself*, *Superboy*, *Deathlok* and various incarnations of *Spider-Man*, while his animation career includes *Ben 10: Alien Force*, *Æon Flux*, *G.I. Joe: Renegades*, *Men In Black* and *Godzilla*.

Dave Stewart coloured art for *Abe Sapien*, *Hellboy*, *The Terminator*, *Spider-Man*, *Green Lantern*, *Star Wars*, *Batman*, *Futurama*, *Planet Of The Apes*, *Daredevil*, *Fables*, *B.P.R.D.*, *Judge Dredd*, *Captain America*, *The Guild*, *Hulk*, *The Escapists*, *The Goon*, *The Sandman* and *The Walking Dead*, as well as Issac Mendez' precognitive art on NBC's *Heroes* on television. In addition, he has worked on another seven Joss Whedon comics projects, namely *Buffy the Vampire Slayer*, *Alien Resurrection*, *Angel*, *Titan A.E.*, *Fray*, *Serenity* and *Sugarshock*. Stewart has won the Eisner Award for Colouring nine times.

Blambot's Nate Piekos has lettered for the likes of *Buffy The Vampire Slayer, The Goon, X-Men, Hulk, Hellboy Animated, Sugarshock, Iron Man, The Terminator, The Guild, X-Force, Aliens, Predator, Alien Versus Predator, Prometheus, Fight Club 2, Howard The Duck, Husbands* and *Dollhouse*.

REVIEW

This story provides an excellent insight into what makes Captain Hammer tick. His unshakeable belief in his own press and his lack of subtlety are perfectly captured. The artwork is suitably heroic and the fight sequence is beautifully handled.

NAME
Moist: Humidity Rising

FIRST RELEASE DATE
December 3, 2008
Released online in *Myspace Dark Horse Presents* Issue #17.

DURATION
8 pages

SYNOPSIS
Moist calls a telephone service to talk about his condition and how it began. The operator hangs up on him. He heads to the park just in time to see Captain Hammer punch Dr. Horrible. He meets the Doctor and is inspired to become a henchman.

FIRSTS & LASTS
First appearance of Moist in comics.

INFORMATION
Plutonium-powered humidifiers may be excessive in their effectiveness.

MOIST
He was born in Freehold, New Jersey in 1981. As a child he was unnaturally dry child with constantly chapped lips. He wore a toy robot helmet to bed. He had no friends at school. At the age of six, his father bought him a USSR made Plutonium-powered humidifier on a trip to Chicago, to remedy his condition. His father set it up in his bedroom and overnight it changed him from a dry and arid to moist and clammy.

As an adult, he had a boring job and lived in an apartment that was bedroom, wardrobe and toilet in one room.

After witnessing Dr. Horrible challenge Captain Hammer, he was inspired to answer an advert to become his henchman. He may be the only applicant. He became Moist.

OTHER CHARACTERS
DR. HORRIBLE
He advertises for Henchmen, offering successful applicants what he describes as "decent pay", despite no previous experience being required. Moist meets him in the park after Captain Hammer punches him.

CAPTAIN HAMMER
Moist witnessed his altercation with Dr. Horrible.

BEST LINES
Moist: "I want to keep talking. I've a lot to talk about. I was born in 1981, Freehold, New Jersey...But Moist was born six years later."
Telephone Operator: "I thought you were Moist."
Moist: "I am. I was born again. Born anew."
Telephone Operator: "Out of a vagina?"

CONTINUITY
Moist's first encounter with Dr Horrible takes place during the Doctor's attempt to weaken Captain Hammer in Be Like Me!

Moist wore a N.J. State Police t-shirt in Act Two and is revealed here to be a New Jersey native.

DEATHS
None.

INFLUENCES & REFERENCES

Moist mentions Jesus. It's probably a reference to Jesus Christ, the noted Bethlehem born carpenter.

MISTAKES

None.

NOTES

Later printed in *Myspace Dark Horse Presents* Volume 3 and *Dr. Horrible And Other Horrible Stories*.

There really is a Freehold, New Jersey.

In medical terms, hypohidrosis is an inability to sweat, whilst hyperhidrosis is excessive sweating. If you say either word quick enough, it sounds like its own antonym.

CREDITS

Script	Zack Whedon
Art	Farel Dalrymple
Colors	Dan Jackson
Letters	Blambot's Nate Piekos

As Seen In *Dr. Horrible's Sing-Along Blog*

Farel Dalrymple has worked on *Fantastic Four*, *The Guild*, *Transmetropolitan*, *Grendel*, *The Wrenchies*, *Omega The Unknown* and his award-winning comics series *Pop Gun War* among others.

Dan Jackson's work in comics includes *Aliens*, *Star Wars*, *Hellboy*, *Hellboy Junior*, *The Guild*, *Conan*, *Planet Of The Apes*, *Buffy The Vampire Slayer*, *Angel & Faith*, *Killjoys*, *Ghost*, *The Terminator*, *The Incredibles* and *Werewolves On The Moon*.

REVIEW

It's great to see Moist take centre stage, but even better to see him as the unlikely recipient of an origin story. We learn the reason for his superpower/medical condition and are shown his first meeting with Dr. Horrible. This is an origin story that subverts the concept with its own take on the science run amok idea and acknowledging the silliness therein.

The artwork isn't altogether comfortable to look at and the likenesses do suffer as well, but the reveal of Moist in tears and the last panel combination of Moist's certain response of "Definitely" to Dr. Horrible's vague "Maybe I'll see you around" and the tear off Henchmen Needed advert are fantastic.

NAME
Penny: "Keep Your Head Up"

FIRST RELEASE DATE
June 4, 2009
Released online in *Myspace Dark Horse Presents* Issue #23

DURATION
8 pages

SYNOPSIS
Penny celebrates her birthday alone, goes on a date and then does her laundry.

FIRSTS & LASTS
The first appearance of Penny in comics and the first appearance of Wingspan in any media.

INFORMATION
United We Stand, How About The Oceans and Animals Are People Too (A.A.P.T.) are all campaign groups.

Jamaica's Cakes is a Los Angeles cake shop.

PENNY
Both her parents are deceased. As a tradition, she spends the evening of her birthday dining with a photo of her them. On this particular birthday, she buys herself a cake from Jamaica's Cakes and Chinese takeout, but gives the former to an old man sleeping in the foyer of her apartment building and the latter to a sickly pigeon that landed on her windowsill. She ends up sticking a candle in a popsicle and eating that.

Her favourite superhero is Elementia.

She is a member of United We Stand, How About The Oceans and Animals Are People Too. Between them and the Caring Hands Homeless Shelter, she doesn't have much time for herself. She goes to the laundromat and becomes aware of Billy for the first time.

DR. HORRIBLE
Penny is in the park when he gets beaten by Captain Hammer. He later attempts to speak to Penny at the laundromat, but mumbles instead.

CAPTAIN HAMMER
Penny is in the park when he beats Dr. Horrible.

OTHER CHARACTERS
DORIS
She works with Penny at the Caring Hands Homeless Shelter.

MAX
He is a homeless man who frequents the Caring Hands Homeless Shelter.

WINGSPAN
He is a male superhero. Wingspan can fly. He recently defeated a disgruntled sixty feet tall robot. He is the favourite superhero of Penny's date.

ELEMENTIA
She is a female superhero. She is Penny's favourite.

BEST LINES
Penny: "Robots. Pssh"
Penny's Date: "The thing was sixty feet tall!"

Penny: "If we lined up all the Styrofoam cups Americans throw away each year how many times do you think it would wrap around the Earth?"

Penny's Date: "Twice?"

Penny: "Four hundred and thirty-six times. If we took all the office paper we throw away we could build a wall twelve feet high that stretches fom New York to Los Angeles."

Penny's Date: "Like to keep the Mexicans out?"

Penny: "Every three and a half seconds someone starves to death."

Penny's date: "Whoa."

Penny: "There are nine hundred and fifty million undernourished people in the world. In Iran a woman can be stoned to death for committing adultery. Superheroes are good for fighting sixty-foot robots for sure, but how often do you see one of those? Where's Wingspan when a little girl goes to sleep hungry or homeless?"

Penny's Date: "...Probably at his headquarters. I've always pictured it as like some underground chamber."

CONTINUITY
Penny is also in the park during Dr Horrible's attempt to weaken Captain Hammer seen in both Be Like Me! and Humidity Rising.

DEATHS
None.

INFLUENCES & REFERENCES
The artwork is very reminiscent of the work of Daniel Clowes.

Jamaica's Cakes really is a Los Angeles cake shop.

Among the many things on the walls of Penny's apartment is one of Andy Warhol's Campbell's Soup Cans.

MISTAKES
None.

NOTES
Later printed in *Myspace Dark Horse Presents* Volume 4 and *Dr. Horrible And Other Horrible Stories*.

Penny's statistics appear to be largely accurate: Americans throw away an estimated 25 billion Styrofoam cups every year (which works out at about 82 cups per person), 4.5 million tons of office paper each year, someone dies every three and a half to four seconds of starvation, by official estimates there were 963 million malnourished people in the world and both men and women found guilty of adultery have been stoned to death in Iran, in 2012 a revised penal code officially ended the practice of stoning in the country, however women have continued to be sentenced to death by stoning as late as 2015.

CREDITS
Script ....Zack Whedon
Art ....Jim Rugg
Colors ....Dan Jackson
Letters ....Nate Piekos

Jim Rugg is responsible for artwork for *The Walking Dead*, *Afrodisiac*, *American Virgin*, *Judge Dredd*, *Madman*, *Fables*, *Wolverine And The X-Men*, *The Guild* and *God Hates Astronauts* and many more.

REVIEW
The idea of a girl who has time for everyone else, but has none left for herself is well explored here. This strip ups the kitchen sink drama quotient and dials back on the superhero elements, quite literally putting it in the background. The artwork lends itself to this expertly. Thankfully Penny's torrent of facts during

her date, never quite crosses over from a woman on a mission to one on a soapbox. The right balance is struck between the tragic and the comic components.

NAME
Dr. Horrible

FIRST RELEASE DATE
November 18, 2009
Released as a special one-shot comic

DURATION
24 pages

SYNOPSIS
Aged eight years old, Billy is inspired by a supervillain's defeat of his favourite superhero. Twenty years later, he takes his first steps to becoming a supervillain himself.

FIRSTS & LASTS
First appearance of Bad Horse in comics. Last appearance of Dr. Horrible, Penny and Moist to date.

INFORMATION
Club Squish was an establishment trading in 1986. It was the site of an encounter between Justice Joe and Mister Maniacal.

Freeze Cream is an age-taunting skin cream.

DR. HORRIBLE
Billy was born in 1978. In 1986, at the age of eight, he was already in the sixth grade. Justice Joe was his hero, until he saw him defeated by Mister Maniacal. He was bullied.

In 2006, as Dr. Horrible he places a microexplosive disguised as a 25 cent coin into every parking meter in the city and planned to detonate them by remote. He accidentally bumps into Captain Hammer, meeting him for the first time. Hammer offers him an autograph, but upon hearing his name inquires whether he is evil and then beats him up.

Billy does his laundry and sees Penny again, when she drops her laundry he helps her pick it up. He lines up in the park for Captain Hammer's autograph, but is punched clear across the park. During the affray, he manages to grab a handful of Hammer's hair.

Dr. Horrible uses the hair to extract Captain Hammer's D.N.A. and six weeks later creates a formula designed to make himself stronger. He also makes an antidote. He injects himself with the formula and despite no visible transformation, it works. He is as strong as Hammer, but it also reduces his mental capacity to the Captain's level. He and Hammer fight. Moist injects him with the antidote. Captain Hammer throws a metal girder at him and the Doctor uses his Transmatter to transport it back to his lab and also partially liquefy it. Dr. Horrible searches his bag of gadgets and discovers his parking meter explosive remote control. He detonates it as he and Moist make their escape.
Dr. Horrible becomes headline news.

PENNY
She does her laundry. Penny is bumped into by another laundromat customer and drops her clothing. Billy helps her pick them up.

CAPTAIN HAMMER
Dr. Horrible runs straight into him, he offers him an autograph and upon discovering that he is evil beats him up, hearing Bad Horse he departs.

Whilst signing autograph in the park, he punches Dr. Horrible clear across the park, but in the affray the Doctor manages to grab a handful of Hammer's hair.

Six weeks later, Dr. Horrible seeks out Captain Hammer for a fight and to the Captain's surprise the Doctor is suddenly as strong as him. They fight. Dr. Horrible detonate an explosive device in every parking meter in the city to assist in their escape.

OTHER CHARACTERS
JUSTICE JOE
Superhero. He is available as an action figure. He was killed in 1986 by Mister Maniacal, weakened by his ray gun and then beaten to death with a pipe. He was Billy's favourite hero, he was disappointed when he witnessed him final fight with Mister Maniacal and ultimately inspired by Maniacal's slaying of Joe.

MISTER MANIACAL
Supervillain. He is available as an action figure. In 1986, he developed a ray gun to weaken Justice Joe and later successfully used it, before killing him with a pipe. He was followed by an angry mob, which then set him on fire. His successful attack on Justice Joe inspired an eight year old Billy to become Dr. Horrible.

BAD HORSE
He stands atop a building, somehow. Captain Hammer attempts to foil him.

MOIST
He has a car, which Dr. Horrible has dubbed the 'Horrible Mobile'. Moist is now henchmanning for Dr. Horrible. Captain Hammer punches Dr. Horrible into the air and he lands on the hood of Moist's car. Moist injects Dr. Horrible with the antidote to his strength formula in an attempt to return his intelligence. It works.

BEST LINES

Mister Maniacal: "Now the world will see that brains will always beat brawn!"
Justice Joe: "Whatever you say Einstein!"
Bystander #1: "What a hilarious made-up name!"
Bystander #2: "He's as witty as he is strong!"

Moist: You want people to follow you, but after Mister Maniacal defeated Justice Joe, he wasn't followed...I mean he was followed, but by a mob that then set him on fire."

CONTINUITY

For the fourth time, we see the autographs in the park Captain Hammer versus Dr. Horrible fight previously seen in the other three comic strips. This strip depicts the moment that Dr. Horrible was inspired to build the freeze ray.

DEATHS

Two: Justice Joe was beaten to death with a pipe by Mister Maniacal. Mister Maniacal was set on fire by an angry mob.

INFLUENCES & REFERENCES

Bad Horse in silhouette resembles the Dark Horse comic logo.

MISTAKES

None.

NOTES

Later printed in *Dr. Horrible And Other Horrible Stories*.

There are approximately 40,000 parking meters in Los Angeles.

CREDITS

Story by ....Zack Whedon
Art ....Joëlle Jones
Colors ....Dan Jackson
Letters .... Blambot's Nate Piekos

Joëlle Jones' artwork has graced *12 Reasons Why I Love Her*, *Spider-Man*, *You Have Killed Me*, *The Girl Who Owned A City*, *Batman '66*, *Troublemaker*, *Superman*, *Fables*, *Madame Frankenstein*, *Fight Club 2* and more.

REVIEW

They say never meet your heroes, and this tale shows that Billy seeing Justice Joe fall from grace and ultimately that the bad guy doesn't need to lose would pave the way for the future we've already seen.

The artwork is great and the likenesses are quite faithful throughout. This is a brilliant origin story and prequel that successfully manages to remain faithful to its predecessor whilst feeling fresh.

The flashback is fantastic, the characterisation is brilliant and dénouement is well earned. You really can't ask for more.⬚

NAME
The Evil League Of Evil

FIRST RELEASE DATE
September 21, 2010
Released in *Dr. Horrible, and Other Horrible Stories*.

DURATION
16 pages

SYNOPSIS
The Council of Champions depart the city leaving open season for the Evil League of Evil.

FIRSTS & LASTS
First appearance of Professor Normal, Tie Die, Dead Bowie, Fury Leika and the Bad Horse Chorus in comics. First slice of Dr. Horrible not to feature Dr. Horrible. Last appearance of Captain Hammer, Bad Horse, Wingspan, Professor Normal, Tie Die, Dead Bowie, Fury Leika and the Bad Horse Chorus to date.

INFORMATION
City Tribune is a local newspaper. One water main supplies half the city.

The Evil League of Evil has an enormous mansion-sized lair built on the edge of a precipice.

The Council of Champions has a spring retreat in Ojai, California, USA.

BAD HORSE
Upon hearing of the Council of Champions' spring retreat, he plots to take advantage of their absence. Bad Horse attacks an art gallery. He can talk, he just presumably chooses not to.

PROFESSOR NORMAL

He has a mechanical left arm that can lift great weight and tear through metal. Professor Normal and Dead Bowie attack a chemical facility and steal a barrel of poison. He attempts to pour it into the city's water supply, but is prevented from doing so by Johnny Snow. He steals actual candy from an actual baby.

FURY LEIKA

She is present when the Evil League of Evil attempts to poison the city's water supply.

TIE DIE

She influences a group of hippies to turn on each other and lures them to the site of a particularly vulnerable water pipe.

DEAD BOWIE

He can hypnotise people to do his bidding. During the Council of Champions' spring retreat, he attacks a deadly chemical facility. He hypnotises an army of hippies to do his digging.

FAKE THOMAS JEFFERSON

He claims to be 267 years old. He claims to be able to understand Bad Horse's whinnies. He claims to have a country home called Monticello. He has the strength to lift a car above his head. He considers himself to be the real Thomas Jefferson. He claims to have had a profound effect on the Second Continental Congress. He renders James Flames unconscious with a quill dart that he throws expertly. He only carries one as he doesn't like to have a lot in his pockets. He wants to serve as the Evil League of Evil's second in command, or vice president if you will.

OTHER CHARACTERS
CAPTAIN HAMMER
He is a member of the Council of Champions. Captain Hammer's command center has a telephone in the shape of a football. He has accidentally torn off a refrigerator door, more than once. He attends the Council of Champions spring retreat.

WINGSPAN
He is a member of the Council of Champions. Wingspan's command center is up in the clouds. He has a logo that incorporates the letter 'w' and a pair of wings. Even when naked, he leaves his mask on. He attends the Council of Champions spring retreat.

ELEMENTIA
She is a member of the Council of Champions. Elementia's command center is behind a waterfall. Her logo is a lower case 'e' with a lightning bolt through it. She attends the Council of Champions spring retreat.

THE NBN NEWSREADERS
One of them is called Steve. The other might be called Kitten (although it could simply be an affectionate nickname).

JOHNNY SNOW
He is a hero, but not a member of the Council of Champions. Snow discovers the Evil League of Evil about to poison the city's water supply and freezes it solid with his ice gun to prevent them. This is mistaken as an act of evil, which impresses the Evil League of Evil and is reported by NBN News as the actions of "evil, ice-themed villain Donnie Snow.

JAMES FLAMES
He is a hero, but not a member of the Council of Champions. Flames has the power of flames and his ill-fitting clothing is

partially burnt. He is knocked out by Fake Thomas Jefferson's quill dart. When Flames awakes he thaws out the frozen water supply and is hailed as a hero by NBN.

SUZIE
She is a reporter for NBN News. Suzie interviews James Flames following his thawing of the city's water supply.

BEST LINES
Captain Hammer: "What normal, not-special people don't realize is that it's tough being fantastic...Sure I've got superstrength, chiselled features, and am just generally superior, but do you know how many refrigerator doors I've torn off by accident?"
Female Superhero: "I hear ya."
Captain Hammer: "But where's my superhero? No one's there to save me in my time of need, you know?"
Cycloptic Superhero: "Totally."
Wingspan: "Well, there's the repair guy."
Captain Hammer: "Sure. But then it's the song and dance of "sometime between noon and five," and meanwhile my ice cream's melting."

Plus bonus marks for the art gallery visitor's line: "And this is...artwork."

CONTINUITY
NBN News reports on "Who's Gay?" again, as they did in Act Three.

This strip is set before Dr. Horrible joins the Evil League of Evil, but Fake Thomas Jefferson claims to be 267 years old, which assuming his calculations are correct means it takes place in 2010.

The Evil League of Evil's plan to poison the water main was considered by Dr. Horrible in *Dr. Horrible's Sing-Along Blog*, Act Two.

DEATHS
None, but Professor Normal does drip at least some poison on the frozen water in the pipe and when James Flames thaws it

INFLUENCES & REFERENCES
Monticello was a plantation owned and designed by the real Thomas Jefferson and built with slave labour in 1772. He was buried on the grounds. It is now UNESCO World Heritage site and a picture of Monticello is on the back of the current five cent coin.

A hacky sack is a round football like bag popular in the 1970s and designed to be kicked and kept up in the air.

MISTAKES
The real Thomas Jefferson's Monticello is actually open between 8:30am and 7pm.

NOTES
In Act One Billy and Penny had yet to make an audible connection, but in this story set before the *Sing-Along Blog* they exchange words.

CREDITS
Story by	Zack Whedon
Art	Scott Hepburn
Colors	Dan Jackson
Letters	Blambot's Nate Piekos

Scott Hepburn has provided art for *Star Wars*, *Captain Marvel*, *The Flash*, *Deadpool*, *Avengers*, *Thundercats* and *Streetfighter*.

REVIEW

This is fantastic . The highlights are many and varied: the artwork is magnificent throughout, the use of Johnny Snow is wonderful, the undercutting it receives with the reveal of James Flames is great, the incredulous stares of the Evil League of Evil at Snow's naiveté finally catches up with their attempt at mass murder are brilliant, the fact that we get not just one, but two examples of the death whinny and the ending is superb.

CHRONOLOGY

Circa 13 Billion Years Ago
The universe is created by the Big Bang (probably).

1743, April 2 (or 13 depending on your choice of calendar)
The Real Thomas Jefferson is born.

1772
Monticello is built as a residence for the Real Thomas Jefferson
[*The Evil League Of Evil*].

1775, May 10
The Second Continental Congress is established. At some point,
the Real Thomas Jefferson is in attendance. The Fake Thomas
Jefferson will claim to have had a profound persuasive effect on
it [*The Evil League Of Evil*].

1781, March 1
The Second Continental Congress is disbanded [*The Evil League
Of Evil*].

1801, March 4
The Real Thomas Jefferson is elected third President of the
United States of America.

1809, March 4
The Real Thomas Jefferson is replaced by the fourth President of
the United States of America.

1826, July 4
The Real Thomas Jefferson dies. Or does he?

1947, January 8
David Bowie is born.

1978
Billy is born [*Dr. Horrible* one-shot comic]

1981
Moist is born in the actual, factual, parturition, sense of the word in Freehold, New Jersey, USA [*Moist: Humidity Rising*].

1986
Mister Maniacal kills Justice Joe as a young Billy looks on [*Dr. Horrible* one-shot comic]

1987
Moist is born in the humidifying reborn sense of the word, when his father returns from Chicago with a plutonium-powered humidifier, which turns his son into the damp and clammy henchman of tomorrow [*Moist: Humidity Rising*].

2000
The Toy Collector by James Gunn is published [*Dr. Horrible's Sing A-Long Blog*, Act Two]

2009, a Friday, Penny's birthday
After a day working at the Caring Hands Homeless Shelter, Penny celebrates her birthday alone in her apartment [*Penny: Keep Your Head Up*]

2009
Dr. Horrible inserts a microexplosive disguised as 25 cent coin into every parking meter in the city, but the detonation is interrupted by Captain Hammer's fist. Who then departs to deal with Bad Horse. Billy takes his Dr. Horrible costume to the laundromat, where he sees Penny and a new report on anniversary of the death of Justice Joe [*Dr. Horrible* one-shot comic]

2009, a Sunday
In a public park, Dr. Horrible attempts to weaken Captain
Hammer with a ray gun he invented, he fails [*Captain Hammer
(Nemesis Of Dr. Horrible): Be Like Me!*], but successfully manages
to grab a handful of the Captain's hair [*Dr. Horrible* one-shot
comic], afterwards he meets Moist who applies to become his
henchman [*Moist: Humidity Rising*]. Penny is also in the park,
she is asked out on a date [*Penny: Keep Your Head Up*].

2009, probably a Wednesday or Saturday
Penny goes on a date which proves to be disappointing and then
heads to the laundromat, where she notices Billy for the first
time [*Penny: Keep Your Head Up*]

2009, six weeks after Sunday
Dr. Horrible synthesizes a strength serum from Captain
Hammer's D.N.A. He seeks out Hammer, takes the serum and
they fight. Upon realising that the serum has also reduced Dr.
Horrible's IQ, Moist administers the antidote. They flee from the
Captain using the parking meter microexplosive as a distraction
[*Dr. Horrible* one-shot comic]

2009, six weeks after Monday
Billy cuts a clipping about the new villain Doctor Horrible out of
the newspaper [*Dr. Horrible* one-shot comic].

2009, Christmas
Captain Hammer beats Dr. Horrible up again [*Dr. Horrible's Sing
A-Long Blog*, Act Two]

2010, Spring
The Council of Champions goes on its spring retreat leaving the
city defenceless. The Evil League of Evil seeks to take advantage

of this, but they are defeated by Johnny Snow [*The Evil League Of Evil*]

2010, a Wednesday
Billy and Penny wash their laundry [*Dr. Horrible's Sing A-Long Blog*, Act One]

2010
Billy conducts his Wonderflonium heist, Captain Hammer intervenes and believes he has foiled Dr. Horrible's plans. Hammer meets Penny [*Dr. Horrible's Sing A-Long Blog*, Act One]

2010, a Saturday
Penny and Captain Hammer go on a date [*Dr. Horrible's Sing A-Long Blog*, Act Two]

2010, a Wednesday
Billy and Penny wash their laundry and talk [*Dr. Horrible's Sing A-Long Blog*, Act Two]

2010, a Saturday
Billy and Penny wash their laundry. Captain Hammer drops by [*Dr. Horrible's Sing A-Long Blog*, Act Two]

2010
The Mayor's dedication ceremony for the new Caring Hands Homeless Shelter takes place. Captain Hammer is the guest of honour. It is attended by Penny and Dr. Horrible. Captain Hammer's speech is interrupted by Dr. Horrible and his freeze ray. With Captain Hammer frozen, Dr. Horrible is free to terrorise the assembled audience. Hammer unfreezes and attempts to shoot Dr. Horrible with the malfunctioning Death Ray. The Death Ray explodes and Penny is killed. Captain Hammer runs away from the scene [*Dr. Horrible's Sing A-Long Blog*, Act Three].

2010 (in the days following the Homeless Shelter incident) Captain Hammer goes into therapy and avoid contact with the media. His fans shift their allegiance and become Dr. Horrible fans. Dr. Horrible joins the Evil League of Evil [*Dr. Horrible's Sing A-Long Blog*, Act Three].

NAME
Commentary! The Musical

FIRST RELEASE DATE
December 19, 2008

SYNOPSIS
The behind the scenes inside scoop on the making of *Dr. Horrible's Sing-Along Blog* in commentary form, with songs.

FIRSTS & LASTS
This is the first time that Neil Patrick Harris plays himself in a work associated with *Dr. Horrible's Sing-Along Blog*.

INFORMATION
In September 2007, AMPTP spokesman Nicholas Counter said "I will grind the writer's guild into a fine paste, snort it up my nose, and cut it with baby powder and sell it to underprivileged kids."

JOSS WHEDON
He made $25 from his actors.

NEIL PATRICK HARRIS
He paid Joss $15 to sing 'Ten Dollar Solo' as a duet. He does magic and played a child doctor. When everybody else abandons the studio, Neil attempts to operate the apparatus unaccompanied. He can tap, but he can't rap.

NATHAN FILLION
He admits to phoning in his performance, but regards himself as better than Neil. Nathan makes 'seven-layer bean dip of the gods' and holds the record on *Ninja Ropes* at 119.7 yards. Neil calls him Frankenstein.

FELICIA DAY

She doesn't discuss her process. Felicia fancies Nathan Fillion. She might have a vestigial tail. Nathan calls her monkey face.

STACY SHIRK

She paid Joss ten dollars to sing 'Ten Dollar Solo' solo, but Neil Patrick Harris interrupts and Stacy runs crying from the room. She returns to sing 'All About Me'.

ZACK WHEDON

He raps and doesn't like musicals. Zack claims to have been drunk since 1991 and involved in the death of a prostitute. He might have played the prince in *The King And I*, Pigpen in a *Charlie Brown* show and sang in *Annie Get Your Gun*. He was the tin man in *The Wizard Of Oz*.

Zack wrote a storyline for Moist that saw him arrested for selling blow at a rest stop and sent to prison. Following his release he taught art to underprivileged children at the local high school, until an old gambling buddy comes to collect.

SIMON HELBERG

He had a song cut from the blog that was all about Moist.

JED WHEDON

He plays *Ninja Ropes* on his phone when alone. Jed texted Steve to get him involved in *Commentary! The Musical*.

MAURISSA TANCHEROEN

She wrote all Penny's lines and songs, as well as singing her part on the demo. Maurissa's father is a nerdy, funny scientist and not a transpo guy. She plays the violin and enjoys math.

STEVE BERG
Jed texted him to ask him to be in *Commentary! The Musical*.
He's not Groupie #67606.7627592.

ROB REINIS
He believes it's all about him. He played the moving guy. The
emotionally moving guy.

MARTI NOXON
She believes it's all about her.

DAVID FURY
He believes it's all about him. He believes he and Marti's talent
to be vast. He's listed last on IMDB.

SONGS
'Commentary!'
Written by Joss Whedon
Performed by the Cast and Writers

'Strike!'
Written by Joss Whedon
Performed by Joss Whedon, Jed Whedon, Zack Whedon and
Maurissa Tancharoen

'Ten Dollar Solo'
Music by Joss Whedon and Jed Whedon
Lyrics by Joss Whedon
Performed by Stacy Shirk and Neil Patrick Harris

'Better Than Neil'
Music by Jed Whedon
Lyrics by Joss Whedon and Jed Whedon
Performed by Nathan Fillion and Maurissa Tancharoen

'The Art'
Written by Joss Whedon
Performed by Felicia Day

'Zack's Rap'
Music by Jed Whedon
Lyrics by Zack Whedon, Jed Whedon, and Maurissa Tancharoen
Performed by Zack Whedon and Maurissa Tancharoen

'Moist'
Written by Jed Whedon
Performed by Simon Helberg

'Ninja Ropes'
Written by Jed Whedon
Performed by Jed Whedon, Neil Patrick Harris, and Nathan Fillion

'All About Me'
Written by Joss Whedon
Performed by Steve Berg, David Fury, Marti Noxon, Rob Reinis, Stacy Shirk, Maurissa Tancharoen and Jed Whedon

'Nobody's Asian In The Movies'
Written by Maurissa Tancharoen and Jed Whedon
Performed by Maurissa Tancharoen

'Heart, Broken'
Written and performed by Joss Whedon

'Neil's Turn'
Written by Joss Whedon
Performed by Neil Patrick Harris

'Commentary!' (Reprise)
Written by Joss Whedon
Performed by Cast and Writers

'Steve's Song'
Music by Jed Whedon
Lyrics by Jed Whedon and Joss Whedon
Performed by Steve Berg

BEST LINES
Neil & Maurissa: "And you'll be dazed by the haze of blazing praise, arrays of ways to rephrase: those were the days."

Zack: "I'm the youngest!"

All: "You've got just one life to fly and dive from place to place, don't ask why a ninja can survive in outer space"

All: "But you're unfazed by the maze of crazy malaise, the lazy phrasing betrays, how well this pays"

CONTINUITY
There are numerous brilliantly timed references to what is happening on screen in *Dr. Horrible's Sing-Along Blog*.

DEATHS
None.

INFLUENCES & REFERENCES
AMPTP stands for the Alliance of Motion Picture and Television Producers.

A lyric in 'Strike' describes lawyers criticism of writer's behaviour "...as convincing as a cockney Dick Van Dyke...", which references his part in *Mary Poppins* (1964).

The same song uses the phrase "let them eat cake", that reflects a disregard for starving peasants and is often attributed to Marie Antoinette (1755-1793), but that first appeared when she was nine years old.

A lyric in 'Ten Dollar Solo' mentions *Fame* (1980), and that its remake (2009) is better than the original. The remake was directed by Kevin Tancharoen, who is Maurissa Tancharoen's brother.

In 'Better Than Neil' the game *Ninja Ropes* is mentioned. It is a real game playable online.

Pope car refers to various Popemobiles used by various Popes since 1976.

The same song also refers to Neil Patrick Harris' Emmy nomination for Outstanding Supporting Actor in a Comedy Series for *How I Met Your Mother*, Nathan Fillion's appearance in computer game *Halo 3* (2007) and Harris' role as the eponymous kid doctor in *Doogie Howser, M.D.* (1989).

Nathan Fillion's claims to having *Kids-In-The-Hall*ness and Pink-Floyd's-*The Wall*ness, allude to a Canadian comedy group formed in 1984 and the eleventh studio album by the English prog rock band Pink Floyd respectively.

Nathan Fillion suggests Purell is the answer to Neil Patrick Harris' stench. It's an instant hand sanitizer which claims to kill 99.99% of most common germs that may cause illness in fifteen seconds.

'Man of Steel' is a nickname traditionally applied to *Superman* (1938).

Nathan Fillion mentions his role as Joey Buchanan in *One Life To Live* (1995-2007). Fillion's Buchananity is unsurpassed.

Felicia Day irritates everyone by repeatedly plugging her webseries, *The Guild* (2007) even its website.

Stanislavski, Strasberg and Streep are three alliterative surnames of Konstantin, Lee and Meryl respectively. Konstantin Stanislavski (1863-1938) was a Russian theatre practitioner, author of *An Actor Prepares* among others and developer of his acting system. Lee Strasberg (1901-1982) was an American theatre practitioner, director of The Actor's Studio, acted in *The Godfather* Part II (1974) and developer of his acting Method. Meryl Streep is an American actress who appeared in *Kramer Versus Kramer* (1979), *Sophie's Choice* (1982), *Postcards From The Edge* (1990), *Adaptation* (2002), *Florence Foster Jenkins* (2016) and many more.

Mr Lipton refers to James Lipton, host of *Inside The Actor's Studio* (1994) and upon which Neil Patrick Harris was a guest.

Red Bull is an energy drink brought to the marketplace in 1987.

Hulu is an American subscription video on demand service launched in 2007.

Harry Wismer (1913-1967) was a sports broadcaster who died after a fall down the stairs.

Ninja Ropes Extreme Version is a real game playable online.

Solitaire is a card game for one player.

IMDb stands for the Internet Movie Database. It was launched in 1990 and features listings of essentially every movie, television show or online musical ever made. Such as http://www.imdb.com/title/tt1227926 and http://www.imdb.com/title/tt1378218.

The Viet Cong was a political organization and army that operated in South Vietnam and Cambodia during the Vietnam War (1955-1975).

"Loving you long time" refers to a phrase used by prostitutes whilst offering their services, most associated with *Full Metal Jacket* (1987)

In 'Heart, Broken', Joss Whedon mentions Homer's *Odyssey*, the 8th Century BCE epic poem, and Charybdis, a mythological creature featured therein.

Comic-Con is a comic convention held annually in San Diego, California since 1970.

Ryan Green was the director of photography

J-Mo is presumably a nickname for Jed Whedon and Maurissa Tancharoen as a couple that echoes that of American singer, actress, dancer, fashion designer, author and producer Jennifer Lopez.

Neil calls Nathan 'Frankenstein', referring to the 1818 novel, *Frankenstein; or, The Modern Prometheus*, by Mary Shelley (1797-1851). It's probably not meant as a compliment.

Hal Holbrook is an actor that became famous for playing Mark Twain in a one-man show. He later appeared in *All the*

President's Men (1976), *Capricorn One* (1978) and *The West Wing* (2001-2002) among many more.

Liza is presumably Liza Minnelli, the actress and singer best known for playing of Sally Bowles in *Cabaret* (1972). Neil with an 'I' alludes to her showcase *Liza With A 'Z': A Concert for Television* (1972).

Neil mentions that the boom guy was great, but he can't remember his name. His name was Michael Kaleta.

In 'Steve's Song', the line "Alive are these hills" alludes to "The hills are alive", the first line of 'The Sound Of Music' the title song of *The Sound Of Music* (1959), while 'Sussudio' is a song by Phil Collins, released as a 1985 single and reached No. 1 on the U.S. Billboard charts.

MISTAKES
David Fury isn't listed last on IMDb, I want him to know that.

NOTES
None.

CREDITS
Cast

Joss Whedon	Himself
Neil Patrick Harris	Himself
Nathan Fillion	Himself
Felicia Day	Herself
Jed Whedon	Himself
Zack Whedon	Himself
Maurissa Tancharoen	Herself
Stacy Shirk	Herself
Steve Berg	Himself
Marti Noxon	Herself

Davd Fury ....Himself
Simon Helberg ....Himself
Rob Reinis ....Himself
Written by ....Maurissa Tancharoen
....Jed Whedon
....Joss Whedon
....Zack Whedon
Produced by ....Jed Whedon
Music by...Jed Whedon
Directed by...Jed Whedon
....Joss Whedon

REVIEW

Commentary! The Musical sees the cast play caricatured versions of themselves, bickering and whinging about the scale of their roles.

They do so in song and what's more really great songs too. Complex melodies and varying styles abound. 'Ten Dollar Solo', 'Better Than Neil', 'Zack's Rap,' 'All About Me', 'Nobody's Asian In The Movies' and 'Steve's Song' are phenomenal songs and deserve to be heard far more widely than this commentary curio could ever allow.

Commentary! The Musical perfectly punctures all the stereotypes of DVD commentaries and is a very funny and insightful piece in its own right.

MERCHANDISE

There is a surprising array of *Dr. Horrible's Sing-Along Blog* merchandise available.

THE DVD

The DVD is region free and contain all three acts of *Dr. Horrible's Sing-Along Blog*, a cast and crew commentary, *Commentary! The Musical*, three making of Dr Horrible featurettes, Evil League Of Evil Application videos, subtitles in English, Spanish, French, German, Wiccan (see below), Japanese and Chinese, English 5. 1 surround sound and widescreen (16x9) picture and a number of Easter Eggs.

The back of the DVD sleeve has "Count the letters U + L + R + D" written in the bottom left. When you insert the DVD the FBI warning is replaced by ELE Warning and briefly a shot of three eggs.

Easter Egg 1 of 3: Choose the Wiccan subtitles from the Languages menu. The last will tell you to "Enter at 9780793529865". Now Google it. Yep. The first result is the sheet music for Mariah Carey's *Music Box* album. Yep. Head over to The Making Of menu and select 'The Music', skip to chapter 3, press enter and you'll see a countdown with a photo of the Wonderflonium Briefcase at its centre. If we "Count the letters U + L + R + D" in Wonderflonium briefcase we get the number 5. Press 5 and enter before the countdown ends for some interviews with the members of the Evil League Of Evil. If you don't manage to press both buttons in time, you will be taken back to the menu screen.

Easter Egg 2 of 3: Watch the What Just Happened? featurette and pay close attention to the credits: certain individual letters have been coloured in yellow. The yellow letters spell out "enteratact2" or "enter at Act 2". Choose 'Play', skip to chapter 6 and press enter to see an Evil League Of Evil countdown screen with Professor Normal's head in the centre. If we "Count the letters U + L + R + D" in Professor Normal's head we get the number 5. Press 5 and enter before the countdown ends and you'll see a behind-the-scenes look at the filming of 'A Man's Gotta Do'.

Easter Egg 3 of 3: Go to the Scene Selections menu for Act II and highlight the chapter 'Moist Dries Up', press enter for a countdown with a photo of Dr. Horrible's head at its centre. If we "Count the letters U + L + R + D" in Dr. Horrible's head we get the number 6. Press 6 and enter during the countdown for a series of outtakes.

Easter Egg 4 of 3: In the Special Features menu highlight 'Teaser Trailer' and press Left and enter for the DVD production credits. They deserve a watch, these people worked hard.

Easter Egg 5 of 3: Illegally rip the DVD and reportedly when you try to watch them you are greeted by a screen that bears the Evil League of Evil logo and reads: "You ripped our DVD? How do you not fear us yet?"

THE BLU-RAY
As far as I can tell the Blu-Ray and the DVD are almost identical, except there is a new menu screen, no Wiccan subtitles and the Easter Eggs are now easily accessible extras.

THE BOOKS
Dr. Horrible's Sing-Along Blog The Book (ISBN: 978-1848568624) Includes behind the scenes information on the conception, creation and production of *Dr. Horrible's Sing-Along Blog*, notes on costumes, contributions from cast and crew, a full script and sheet music and the script (but not sheet music) for *Commentary! The Musical*.

Myspace Dark Horse Presents Volume 2 (ISBN: 978-1595822482)
Includes *Captain Hammer (Nemesis Of Dr. Horrible): Be Like Me!*

Myspace Dark Horse Presents Volume 3 (ISBN: 978-1595823274)
Includes *Moist: Humidity Rising*.

Myspace Dark Horse Presents Volume 4 (ISBN: 978-1595824059)
Includes *Penny: Keep Your Head Up*.

Dr. Horrible And Other Horrible Stories (ISBN: 978-1-59582-577-3)
Includes *Captain Hammer: Be Like Me!*, *Moist: Humidity Rising*, *Penny: Keep Your Head Up*, the *Dr. Horrible* one-shot and an exclusive story: *The Evil League Of Evil*.

Supervillain!: An Unautorised And Unofficial Guide To The World Of Dr. Horrible's Sing-Along-Blog (ISBN: 978-1980904823)
A peerless reference work. Songs will be sung of its virtues.

THE SOUNDTRACKS
All fourteen songs with a duration of 24:45 from *Dr. Horrible's Sing-Along Blog* were released both on CD and download, while *Commentary! The Musical* was made available for download in its entirety with the dialogue between songs included as separate tracks and 'Zack's Rap' renamed 'The Rap' for some reason.

THE STATUES
You too can adorn your home with a statue of Penny doing her washing or Dr. Horrible brandishing his freeze ray.

THE REST
The interest is awash with T-Shirts, badges, stickers, posters, etc featuring images and quotes from *Dr. Horrible's Sing-Along Blog*

some official, some not, and so an exhaustive list would be instantly out of date.

▯

ONLINE
Official website
http://www.drhorrible.com

Van Remote
http://thesoftwire.com/horrible_remote.html

Wiki
http://drhorrible.wikia.com

Joss Whedon
Twitter @Joss and http://savetheday.vote

Neil Patrick Harris
He tweets as @ActuallyNPH, while his Instagram is
www.instagram.com/nph

Nathan Fillion
twitter as @NathanFillion

Felicia Day
http://feliciaday.com and she tweets from @feliciaday

Simon Helberg
He twitters as @simonhelberg

Nick Towne
He's a twitterer: @RogueRock

Jed Whedon
He tweets as @jedwhedon and his music is available at
https://jedwhedon.bandcamp.com

Zack Whedon
@ZDubDub on twitter

Maurissa Tancheroen
Her twitterings are at @MoTancheroen

Marti Noxon
She tweets at @martinoxon

David Fury
davidfury.com and @TheDavidFury on the twitter.

Stacy Shirk
http://www.stacyshirk.com

Dobber was provided by Phil's Animal Rentals
http://philsanimalrentals.com

Jamaica's Cakes
www.jamaicascakes.com

Eric Canete
http://www.kahnehteh.blogspot.co.uk

Blambot's Nate Piekos
http://www.blambot.com

Farel Dalrymple
http://fareldalrymple.com

Jim Rugg
http://jimrugg.blogspot.co.uk.

Felicia Day's The Guild webseries
http://watchtheguild.com.

Ninja Ropes is playable at:
www.sarkscape.com/games/iphone/ninja-ropes

Ninja Ropes Extreme version is playable at:
www.sarkscape.com/games/iphone/ninja-ropes-extreme⬚

SEE YOU AT THE AFTERMATH

The day after the debut of Act III, something momentous happened: all three acts were taken offline. It doesn't seem like much, but it showed that you could make something available online and still control it.

They became available again on July 28, and then spread to various other online services, including iTunes, Hulu, Netflix and YouTube. When all three acts were made available on iTunes for the UK and Australia, and they were the number one television season for five weeks in a row.

The linear media paid attention and *Dr. Horrible's Sing-Along Blog* garnered Joss Whedon his first-ever Emmy win, despite a long and critically acclaimed career as a writer, director and producer of many television shows and also the fact that it did not actually air on television. *Time* magazine named *Dr. Horrible's Sing-Along Blog* the fourth best television series of 2008, again despite the fact that it was created for the Internet and had not appeared on television.

Other awards and accolades followed. The *Sing-Along Blog* was nominated in the 2008 Constellation Awards for Best Science Fiction Film, TV Movie, or Mini-Series, while Neil Patrick Harris received a nomination for Best Male Performance in a 2008 Science Fiction Film, TV Movie, or Mini-Series. Both lost out, to *Transformers* and David Tennant respectively.

At the 2009 Streamy Awards, it won the Audience Choice Award for Best Web Series, Best Directing for a Comedy Web Series and Best Writing for a Comedy Web Series, Best Editing, Best Cinematography and Best Original Music. In potentially awkward circumstances both Neil Patrick Harris and Nathan Fillion were nominated for Best Male Actor in a Comedy Web Series. Harris won. Felicia Day won in the Best Female equivalent category, but for *The Guild*, which beat *Dr. Horrible's Sing-Along Blog* for Best Comedy Web Series.

In the same year it won the Hugo Award for Best Dramatic Presentation, Short Form and the People's Choice Award for Favorite Online Sensation.

On October 9, 2012, all three acts made their television broadcast debut at 9pm on The CW in an omnibus edition, edited to 42 minutes to allow for advertising.

In less good news, the Universal back lot used for the alley scene and for Captain Hammer's dramatic entrance in Act One, was destroyed in a fire at the studio in 2008.

Dr. Horrible's Sing-Along Blog has tapped into a rich seam of pop-culture. It was referenced in television shows as varied as *Jeopardy!* (2010), *The Cleveland Show* (2011) and *Psych* (2014), not to mention those starring *Sing-Along Blog* alumni like *The Legend Of Neil* (2009), *Neil's Puppet Dreams* (2012), *Castle* (2014) and *The Big Bang Theory* (2015).

Joss Whedon told Paleyfest that he had made more money for *Dr. Horrible's Sing-Along Blog* than he did from *Marvel's The Avengers* (2012).

In 2015, when asked which project she had found the most fun to film, Felicia Day said "Probably *Dr. Horrible*, it was kind of a turning point in web content that hasn't even been realised now. It was these fancy people, 'fancy' because they are awesome, from TV, and they decided to make something essentially in their backyards and finance it themselves for the Internet. It really was the first thing to push Hollywood to see the web as legitimate, as far as where you could [share] content. It was such a phenomenon. To this day, I meet people who are cosplaying as

Dr. Horrible. Just the process of creating a family and creating something that affected so many people, maybe turned the tide of a whole industry? I'm so grateful to be a part of it."

It seems safe to say that *Dr. Horrible's Sing-Along Blog* was the best thing to come of the writer's strike.

THE FUTURE

Talk of a sequel to *Dr Horrible's Sing-Along Blog* seemed inevitable, because of course we want more. When asked if we could expect to see a *Dr. Horrible II*, Joss Whedon paused before slowly saying "The thing that you have to understand is yes."

Nathan Fillion told The TV Addict that he knows the title of the sequel, but is unwilling to reveal it at this time. He went on to say "It's awesome, so much so that when you hear this new title, you'll get that same rush and feeling of excitement you did when you heard about the first *Dr. Horrible Sing-Along Blog*. It will boil your blood a little bit."

When asked about the status of a sequel, Joss Whedon told the Oxford Union in December of 2015: "The status is that it's in stasis...everybody is very, very busy. Three of the writers had babies, this year, as well as from making movies and running TV shows. Actually the only one that's available is me. But we did come up with a plot...about five minutes after we finished the first one. And we wrote several songs. And then it all just kind of ground to a halt as these as things do. Where it remains, I think we all intend to get back on that horse at some point, but I have absolutely no idea when. So it was not just a rumour. There is not a completed script, that is so much poppycock, but there are some very good songs, and a few crappy ones."

Seven months later, he told San Diego Comic Con the setting for a sequel: "It takes place after the events of the first. It's in the time when Dr. Horrible has basically taken over the world and is really happy. That lasts about three minutes."

There has been less talk of a second *Dr. Horrible* since then, but there is still hope. Anyone else hoping there is another writer's strike...?

ACKNOWLEDGEMENTS

Firstly, an enormous thank you to my wonderful wife, Sarah, for her unending support, enthusiasm and ability to read.

I owe a thank you to my sister, Beth, who actually bought the DVD for me before it was available in the UK and to the guy in New York who sold it to her, who had absolutely no idea what it was.

Thanks to Philip and Susan Holmes, Jane Vassiliadis, Keith Topping, Abigail Gallagher, Vera Chok, Skippy QSB, Zeagus and Ella Day. To Kate, Joe, Rose and Anna Bennett for the pencil and ruler combination gift and surprisingly to my toughest critic: Nahla, our cat, who walked across the keyboard deleting huge tracts of text as she went. When I rewrote those elements they were better, every damn time.

It would be remiss of me not to thank the cast and crew of both Dr. Horrible's Sing-A-Long Blog and Commentary! The Musical, as well as those responsible for the comic strips as well.

And lastly, but not in the slightest bit leastly, thank you to you. The you that is you.

ABOUT THE AUTHOR

David Black has written articles, sketches and scripts for *Noiseless Chatter*, *Cult Britannia*, *Behind The Bike Shed*, *Newsrevue*, *Outside In* and Hat Trick TV's YouTube channel, *Bad Teeth*. In an act of extreme arrogance, he was forced to reinterpret *The Cherry Orchard* and write new Chekhov dialogue. He blogs a blog at davewrotethis.blogspot.co.uk and tweets like a twit as @davetweetedthis. He is the author of *SUPERVILLAIN!: An Unauthorised and Unofficial Guide to the world of Dr. Horrible's Sing-A-Long Blog*.

COMING SOON...

BIG
DAMN
HEROICS

An Unauthorised and Unofficial Guide to
Firefly and *Serenity*

COMING SOON...

SHIPWRECKED
AND
COMATOSE

An Unauthorised and Unofficial Guide to
Red Dwarf

Printed in Great Britain
by Amazon